THE DALETH EFFECT

was the key to the stars—and Israeli scientist Arnie Klein, its discoverer, knew that the great powers of the world would stop at nothing to control it. Arnie "defected" to tiny, tough Denmark in the hope of being able to carry on his work peacefully.

A dramatic "impossible" rescue of stranded Russian astronauts by a spacegoing submarine breaks the news to the world, and the squeeze play is on—with Arnie and his adopted country the focus of espionage, blackmail, and frank menace, culminating in the first act of space piracy and a bitterly ironic finale.

Also by Harry Harrison

CAPTIVE UNIVERSE
THE DEATHWORLD TRILOGY

THE DALETH EFFECT

HARRY HARRISON

A BERKLEY MEDALLION BOOK
published by
BERKLEY PUBLISHING CORPORATION

Tilgenet
Svend Dragsted

Copyright © 1970, by Harry Harrison

All rights reserved

Published by arrangement with the author's agent
Originally published by G. P. Putnam's Sons

All rights reserved which includes the right
to reproduce this book or portions thereof in
any form whatsoever. For information address

Berkley Publishing Corporation
200 Madison Avenue
New York, N.Y. 10016

SBN 425-03649-9

BERKLEY MEDALLION BOOKS are published by
Berkley Publishing Corporation
200 Madison Avenue
New York, N.Y. 10016

BERKLEY MEDALLION BOOK ® TM 757,375

Printed in the United States of America

Berkley Medallion Edition, DECEMBER, 1977

SECOND PRINTING

THE DALETH EFFECT

1

TEL-AVIV

The explosion that blew out the west wall of the Physics Laboratory of the University of Tel-Aviv did little real harm to Professor Arnie Klein who was working there at the time. A solid steel workbench protected him from the blast and flying debris, though he was knocked down and cut his cheek as he fell. He was understandably shaken as he climbed to his feet again, blinking at the blood on his fingertips where he had touched his face. The far side of the laboratory was just rubble and twisted wreckage, with wreaths of dust or smoke curling up from it.

Fire! The thought of this stirred him to motion. The apparatus had been destroyed, but his records of the experiment and his notes might still be saved. He tugged wildly at the drawer, bent and warped by the blast, until it squealed open. There it was, a thin file folder, a few weeks work—but how important. Next to it a worn folder, fifteen centimeters thick, six years of concentrated labor. He pulled them both out, and since the opening in the wall was close at hand, he went out that way. His records must be made secure first; that was the most important thing.

The pathway here at the back of the building was seldom used, and was deserted now in the breathless heat of the afternoon. This was a shortcut that had been physically impossible to reach from the laboratory before, but now led directly to the faculty dormitory close by. The file would be safe in his room—that was a very good idea. He hurried there, as fast as one can hurry when the dry, furnace-like wind of the khamsin is blowing. Because he was already deep in thought he did not realize that his movements were completely unobserved.

Arnie Klein appeared slow-witted to many people, but this

was only because he was constitutionally unable to follow more than one train of thought at a time, and he had to chew this thought out with methodical thoroughness until every drop of nourishment had been extracted. His mind worked with meticulous precision and ground incredibly fine. Only this unique ability had kept him firmly on this line of reasoning for six years, a complicated chain of mathematical supposition based only upon a gravimetric anomaly and a possible ambiguity in one of Einstein's basic field theory equations.

Now his mind was occupied with a new train of speculation, one he had considered before, but which the explosion had now proven to be a strong possibility. As usual, when deeply involved in thought, his body performed routine operations with, in truth, his conscious mind being completely unaware of them. His clothing was dusty from climbing the debris, as were his hands, and there was blood on his face. He stripped and automatically took a shower, cleaned the cut and applied a small bandage. Only when he began to dress again did his conscious mind intervene. Instead of putting on clean shorts, he took the trousers of his lightweight suit from their hanger and slipped them on. He put a tie in the jacket pocket and draped the jacket across a chair. After this he stopped, in silence for some minutes, while he worked out the logical conclusions of this new idea. A neat, gray-haired man in his early fifties, looking very ordinary, if one made allowance for the fact that he stood for ten minutes, unblinking and motionless, until he reached that conclusion.

Arnie was not sure yet what would be the wisest thing, but he knew what the alternative possibilities were. Therefore he opened his attaché case, still on the dresser where he had put it upon his return from the Belfast Physical Congress the previous week, that contained a book of Thomas Cook & Sons traveler's checks. It was very full because he had thought he would have to pay for his airplane tickets and be reimbursed, but instead the tickets had arrived prepaid. Into the attaché case he put the file folder and his passport, with its visas still in effect; nothing else. Then, with his jacket folded neatly over his arm and carrying the attaché case, he went down the stairs and walked toward the waterfront. Less than a minute later two excited students ran, sweating and breathless, up to his room and hammered on the door.

The khamsin blew with unobstructed relentlessness once he was away from the protection of the campus buildings, drawing the moisture from his body. At first Arnie did not notice this but, in Dizengoff Road, passing the cafés, he became aware of the dryness in his mouth and he turned into the nearest doorway. It was the Casit, a bohemian, Left Bank sort of place, and no one in the variegated crowd even noticed him as he sat at a small table and sipped his *gazos*.

It was there that his chain of thought unreeled to its full length and he made up his mind. In doing this he was completely unaware of any outside influences, and had no idea that an alarmed search was being carried out for him, that waves of consternation were spreading out from the epicenter of the university. At first it had been thought that he was buried under the debris caused by the mysterious explosion, but rapid digging disproved that idea. Then it was discovered that he had been in his room; his soiled clothing was found, as well as traces of blood. No one knew what to believe. Had he been hurt and was he wandering in shock? Had he been abducted? The search widened, though it certainly never came near the Casit café. Inside, Arnie Klein stood up, carefully counted out enough *prutot* coins to pay for his drink, and left.

Once again luck was on his side. A taxi was letting out a fare at Rowal's, the sophisticated café next door, and Arnie climbed in while the door was still open.

"Lydda Airport," he said, and listened patiently while the driver explained that he was going off duty, that he would need more petrol, then commented unfavorably on the weather and a few other items as well. The negotiations that followed were swift because, now that he had come to a decision, Arnie realized that speed would avoid a great deal of unpleasantness.

As they started toward the Jerusalem road two police cars passed them, going in the opposite direction at a tremendous pace.

2

COPENHAGEN

The hostess had to tap his arm to get his attention.

"Sir, would you please fasten your seat belt. We'll be landing in a few minutes."

"Yes, of course," Arnie said, fumbling for the buckle. He saw now that the seat belt and no smoking signs were both lit.

The flight had passed very quickly for him. He had vague memories of being served dinner, although he could not remember what it was. Ever since taking off from Lydda Airport he had been absorbed in computations that grew out of that last and vital experiment. The time had passed very swiftly for him.

With slow grandeur, the big 707 jet tipped up on one wing in a stately turn and the Moon moved like a beacon across the sky. The clouds below were illuminated like a solid yet strangely unreal landscape. The airliner dropped, sped above the nebulous surface for a short time, then plunged into it. Raindrops traced changing pathways across the outside of the window. Denmark, dark and wet, was somewhere down below. Arnie saw that his notebook, the open page covered with scribbled equations, was on the table before him. He put it into his breast pocket and closed the table. Points of light appeared suddenly through the rain and the dark waters of the Oresund streamed by beneath them. A moment later the runway appeared and they were safely down in Kastrup Airport.

Arnie waited patiently until the other passengers had shuffled by. They were Danes for the most part, returning from sunshine holidays, sunreddened faces glowing as though about to explode. They clutched straw sacks and Oriental souvenirs—wooden camels, brass plates, exfoliating rugs—and each had the minuscule tax-free bottle of alcoholic spirits that their watchful government permitted them to bring in. Arnie went last, paces behind the others. The cockpit door was open as he passed, revealing a dim hutch incredibly jammed with shining dials and switches. The captain, a big blond man with an awe-inspiring jaw, smiled at him as he passed. *Capt. Nils Hansen* the badge above his gold wings read.

"I hope you enjoyed the flight," he said in English, the international language of the airways.

"Yes indeed, thank you. Very much." Arnie had a rich British-public-school accent, entirely out of keeping with his appearance. But he had spent the war years at school in England, at Winchester, and his speech was marked for life.

All of the other passengers were queued up at the customs booths, passports ready. Arnie almost joined them until he remembered that his ticket was written through to Belfast and that he had no Danish visa. He turned down the glass-walled corridor to the transit lounge and sat on one of the black leather and chrome benches while he thought, his attaché case between his legs. Staring unseeing into space he considered his next steps. In a few minutes he had reached a decision, and he blinked and looked about. A police officer was tromping solidly through the lounge, massive in his high leather boots and wide cap. Arnie approached him, his eyes almost on a level with the other's silver badge.

"I would like to see the chief security officer here, if you would."

The officer looked down, frowning professionally.

"If you will tell me what the matter is . . ."

"Dette kommer kun mig og den vagthavende officer ved. Sa ma jeg tale med han?"

The sudden, rapid Danish startled the officer.

"Are you Danish?" he asked.

"It does not matter what my nationality is," Arnie continued in Danish. "I can tell you only that this is a matter of national security and the wisest thing for you to do now would be to pass me over to the man who is responsible for these matters."

The officer tended to agree. There was something about

the matter-of-factness of the little man's words that rang of the truth.

"Come with me then," he said, and silently led the way along a narrow balcony high above the main airport hall, keeping a careful eye open so that the stranger with him made no attempt to escape to the rain-drenched freedom of the Kastrup night.

"Please sit down," the security officer said when the policeman had explained the circumstances. He remained seated behind his desk while he listened to the policeman, his eyes, examining Arnie as though memorizing his description, staring unblinkingly through round-paned, steel-framed glasses.

"*Lojtnant Jorgensen,*" he said when the door had closed and they were alone.

"Arnie Klein."

"Ma jeg se Deres pas?"

Arnie handed over his passport and Jorgensen looked up, startled, when he saw it was not Danish.

"You are an Israeli then. When you spoke I assumed . . ." When Arnie didn't answer the officer flipped through the passport, then spread it open on the bare desk before him.

"Everything seems to be in order, Professor. What can I do for you?"

"I wish to enter the country. Now."

"That is not possible. You are here in transit only. You have no visa. I suggest you continue to your destination and see the Danish Consul in Belfast. A visa will take one day, two at the most."

"I wish to enter the country now, that is why I am talking to you. Will you kindly arrange it. I was born in Copenhagen. I grew up no more than ten miles from here. There should be no problem."

"I am sure there won't be." He handed back the passport. "But there is nothing that can be done here, now. In Belfast . . ."

"You do not seem to understand." Arnie's voice was as impassive as his face, yet the words seemed charged with meaning. "It is imperative that I enter the country now, tonight. You must arrange something. Call your superiors. There is the question of dual nationality. I am as much a Dane as you are."

"Perhaps." There was an edge of exasperation to the lieutenant's voice now. "But I am not an Israeli citizen and you are. I am afraid you must board the next plane . . ."

His words trickled off into silence as he realized that the other was not listening. Arnie had placed his attaché case on his knees and snapped it open. He took out a thin address book and flipped carefully through it.

"I do not wish to be melodramatic, but my presence here can be said to be of national importance. Will you therefore place a call to this number and ask for Professor Ove Rude Rasmussen. You have heard of him?"

"Of course, who hasn't? A Nobel prize winner. But you cannot disturb him at this hour . . ."

"We are old friends. He will not mind. And the circumstance is serious enough."

It was after one in the morning and Rasmussen growled at the phone like a bear woken from hibernation.

"Who is that? What's the meaning . . . *Sa for Satan!* . . . is that really you, Arnie. Where the devil are you calling from? Kastrup?" Then he listened quietly to a brief outline of the circumstances.

"Will you help me then?" Arnie asked.

"Of course! Though I don't know what I can possibly do. Just hold on, I'll be there as soon as I can pull some clothes on."

It took almost forty-five minutes and Jorgensen felt uncomfortable at the silence, at Arnie Klein staring, unseeing, at the calendar on the wall. The security officer made a big thing of snapping open a package of tobacco, of filling his pipe and lighting it. If Arnie noticed this he gave no sign. He had other things to think about. The security officer almost sighed with relief when there was a quick knocking on the door.

"Arnie—it really is you!"

Rasmussen was like his pictures in the newspapers; a lean, gangling man, his face framed by a light, curling beard, without a moustache. They shook hands strongly, almost embracing, smiles mirrored on each other's faces.

"Now tell me what you are doing here, and why you dragged me out of bed on such a filthy night?"

"It will have to be done in private."

"Of course." Ove looked around, noticing the officer for the first time. "Where can we talk? Someplace secure?"

"You can use this office if you wish. I can guarantee its security." They nodded agreement, neither seemingly aware of the sarcastic edge to his words.

Thrown out of his own office—what the *hell* was going on? The lieutenant stood in the hall, puffing angrily on his pipe and tamping the coal down with his calloused thumb, until the door was flung open ten minutes later. Rasmussen stood there, his collar open and a look of excitement in his eyes. "Come in, come in!" he said, and almost pulled the security officer into the room, barely able to wait until the door was closed again.

"We must see the Prime Minister at once!" Before the astonished man could answer he contradicted himself. "No, that's no good. Not at this time of night." He began to pace, clenching and unclenching his hands behind his back. "Tomorrow will do for that. We have to first get you out of here and over to my house." He stopped and stared at the security officer.

"Who is your superior?"

"Inspector Anders Krarup but—"

"I don't know him, no good. Wait, your department, the Minister . . ."

"Herr Andresen."

"Of course—Svend Andresen—you remember him, Arnie?"

Klein considered, then shook his head *no*.

"Tiny Anders, he must be well over six feet tall. He was in the upper form when we were at Krebs' Skole. The one who fell through the ice on the Sortedamso."

"I never finished the term. That was when I went to England."

"Of course, the bastard Nazis. But he'll remember you, and he'll take my word for the importance of the matter. We'll have you out of here in an hour, and then a glass of *snaps* into you and you into bed."

It was a good deal more than an hour, and it took a visit by a not-too-happy Minister Andresen, and a hurriedly roused aide, before the matter was arranged. The small office was filled with big men, and the smell of damp wool and cigar smoke, before the last paper was stamped and signed. Then Lieutenant Jorgensen was finally alone, feeling tired and more than a little puzzled by the night's events, his head still filled with the Minister's grumbled advice to him, after taking him aside for a moment.

"Just forget the whole thing, that's all you have to do. You have never heard of Professor Klein and to your knowledge he did not enter the country. That is what you will say no matter *who* asks you."

Who indeed? What was all the excitement about?

3

"I really don't want to see them," Arnie said. He stood by the high window looking out at the park next to the university. The oak trees were beginning to change color already; fall came early to Denmark. Still, there was an excitement to the scene with the gold leaves and dark trunks against the pale northern sky. Small puffs of white clouds moved with stately grace over the red-tiled roofs of the city; students hurried along the paths to classes.

"It would make things easier for everyone if you would," Ove Rasmussen said. He sat behind his big professor's desk in his book-lined professor's office, his framed degrees and awards like heraldic flags on the wall behind him. Now he leaned back in his deep leather chair, turned sideways to watch his friend by the window.

"Is it that important?" Arnie asked, turning about, hands jammed deep into the pockets of the white laboratory coat. There were smears of grease on the sleeve and a brown-rimmed hole in the cuff where a soldering iron had burned through.

"I'm afraid it is. Your Israeli associates are very anxious to find out what happened to you. I understand they traced your movements through a cab driver. They have discovered that you flew by SAS to Belfast—but that you never arrived there. Since the only stopover was here in Copenhagen it was rather hard to conceal your whereabouts. Though I hear that the airport people did give them a very hard time for a while."

"That Lieutenant Jorgensen must have earned his salary."

"He did indeed. He was so bullheaded that there was almost an international incident before the Minister of State admitted that you were here. Now they insist upon talking to you."

"Why? I am a free man. I can go where I please."

"Tell them that. Dark hints about kidnapping have been dropped . . ."

"What! Do they think that the Danes are *Arabs* or something like that?"

Ove laughed and twisted about in his chair as Arnie stamped over and stood before the desk.

"No, nothing like that," he said. "They know—unofficially of course—that you came here voluntarily and that you are unharmed. But they are very curious as to *why* you have come here, and they are not going to go away until they have some answers. There is an official commission right now in the Royal Hotel. They say they will make a statement to the press if they don't see you."

"I do not want that to happen," Arnie said, worried now.

"None of us does. Which is why they want you to meet the Israelis and tell them that you are doing fine and they can take the next flight out. You don't have to tell them any more than that."

"I do not *want* to tell them any more than that. Who have they sent?"

"Four people, but I think three of them are just yes men. I was with them most of the morning, and the only one who really mattered was a General Gev . . ."

"Good God! Not him."

"You know him?"

"Entirely too well. And he knows me. I would rather talk to anyone else."

"I'm afraid you're not getting that chance. Gev is outside right now waiting to see you. If he doesn't talk to you he says he is going straight to the press."

"You can believe him. He learned his fighting in the desert. The best defense is a good offense. You had better show him in here and get it over with. But don't leave me alone with him for more than fifteen minutes. Any more than that and you may find that he has talked me into going back with him."

"I doubt that." Ove stood and pointed to his chair. "Sit here and keep the desk between you. It gives one a feeling of power. Then he'll have to sit on my student-chair there, which is hard as flint."

"If it were a cactus he would not mind," Arnie said, depressed. "You do not know him the way I do."

There was silence after the door closed. An occasional shout from the students outside penetrated the double glass window, but only faintly. Inside the room the ticking of the tall Bornholm clock could be clearly heard. Arnie stared, unseeing, at his folded hands on the desk before him and wondered what to do about Gev. He had to tell him as little as possible.

"It's a long distance to Tel-Aviv," a voice said in guttural Hebrew and Arnie looked up, blinking, to see that Gev was already inside the room and had closed the door behind him. He was in civilian clothes but wore them, straight-backed, like a uniform. His face was tanned, lined, dark as walnut: the long scar that cut down his check from his forehead pulled the corner of his mouth into a perpetual half-grin.

"Come in, Avri, come in. Sit down."

Gev ignored the invitation, stamping across the room, on parade, to stand over Arnie, scowling down at him as though he had been inspected and found wanting.

"I've come to take you home, Arnie. You are one of our leading scientists and your country needs you."

There was no vacillation, no appeal to Arnie's emotions, to his friends or relations. General Gev had issued an order, in the same voice that had commanded the tanks, the jets, the soldiers into combat. He was to be obeyed. Arnie almost rose from his chair and followed him out, so positive was the command. Yet he only stirred uncomfortably in the chair. His decision had been made and nothing could be done about it.

"I am sorry, Avri. I am here and I am going to stay here."

Gev stood, glowering down on him, his arms at his sides but his fingers curved, as though ready to reach out and grasp and pull Arnie bodily to his feet. Then, in instant decision, he turned and sat down in the waiting chair and crossed his legs. His frontal assault had been repulsed; he turned the flank and prepared to attack in a more vulnerable area. Never taking his eyes from Arnie he took a vulgarly large gold cigarette case from his pocket and snapped it open. The flag of the United Arab Republic was set into the case in enamel, the two green stars picked out with emeralds. A bullet hole punched neatly through the case.

"There was an explosion in your laboratory," Gev said. "We were concerned. At first we thought you were dead, then injured—then kidnapped. Your friends have been very concerned . . ."

"I did not mean them to be."

". . . and not only your friends, your government. You are an Israeli, and the work you do is for Israel. A file is missing. Your work has been stolen from your country."

Gev lighted a cigarette and drew deeply on it, cupping the burning end in his hand, automatically, the way a soldier does. His eyes never left Arnie's face and his own face was as expressionless as a mask, with only those accusing eyes peering through. Arnie opened his hands wide in a futile gesture, then clasped them before him once again.

"The work has not been stolen. It is my work and I took it with me when I left. When I left voluntarily, to come here. I am sorry that you . . . think ill of me. But I did what I had to do."

"What was this work?" The question was cold and sharp, and cut deep.

"It was . . . my work." Arnie felt outmaneuvered, outfought, and could only retreat into silence.

"Come now, Arnie. That's not quite good enough. You are a physicist and your work has to do with physics. You had no explosives, yet you managed to blow up some thousands of pounds worth of equipment. What have you invented?"

The silence lengthened, and Arnie could only stare miserably at his clenched hands, his knuckles whitening with the pressure. Gev's words pulled at him, relentlessly.

"What is this silence? You can't be afraid? You have nothing to fear from Eretz Israel, your homeland. Your friends, your work, your very life is there. You buried your wife there. Tell us what is wrong and we will help you. Come to us and we will aid you."

Arnie's words fell like cold stones into the silence.

"I . . . cannot."

"You have to. You have no other choice. You are an Israeli and your work is Israeli. We are surrounded by an ocean of enemies and every man, every scrap of material is vital for our existence. You have discovered something powerful, something that will aid our survival. Would you remove it and see us all perish—the cities and the synagogues leveled to be a desert again? Is that what you want?"

"You know that I do not! Gev, let me be, get out of here and go back . . ."

"That I *won't* do. I won't let you be. If I am the voice of your conscience, so be it. Come home. We will welcome you. Help us as we helped you."

"*No!* That is the thing I cannot do!" The words were pulled from his body, a gasp of pain. He went on quickly, as though the dam to his feelings had been broken and he could not stop.

"I have discovered something—I will not tell you how, why, what it is—a force. Call it a force, something that is perhaps more powerful, or could be more powerful than anything we know today. A force that can be used for good or evil because it is by nature that sort of thing, if I can develop it, and I think I can. I want it used for good—"

"Israel is evil! You dare suggest that?"

"No, hear me out, I did not say that. I mean only that Israel is the pawn of the world with no one on their side. Oil. The Arabs have the oil, and the Soviets and the Americans want it and will play any dirty game to get it. No one cares for Israel, except the Arabs who wish to see her destroyed, and the world powers who also wish they could find a way to destroy her quietly, the thorn in their sides. Oil. War will come, something will happen, and if you have my—if you had *this*, what we are talking about, it would be used for destruction. You would use it, with tears in your eyes perhaps, but you would use it—and that would be absolute evil."

"Then," General Gev said, in a voice so low it was scarcely audible, "from pride, personal ambition, you will withhold this force and see your country perish? In your supreme egocentricity you think yourself more fit to make major policy decisions than the elected representatives of the people. You place yourself on a pillar. You are unique. Better able to decide the important issues than all the lesser mortals of the world. You must believe in absolute tyranny—*your* tyranny. In your arrogance you become a little Hitler . . ."

"Shut up!" Arnie shouted hoarsely, half rising from the chair. There was silence. He sat down again, slowly, aware that his face was flushed, a pulse hammering like a rivet gun in his temple. It took a great effort to speak calmly.

"All right. You are correct in what you say. If you wish to say that I no longer believe in democracy, say it. In this matter I don't. I have made the decision and the responsibility is mine alone. To myself, perhaps as an excuse, I prefer to think of it as a humane act . . ."

"Mercy killing is also humane," Gev said in a toneless voice.

"You are right, of course. I have no excuses. I have acted willfully and I accept the responsibility."

"Even if Israel is destroyed through your arrogance?"

Arnie opened his mouth to answer, but there were no words. What could be said? Gev had him hemmed in from all sides, his retreat was cut off, his defenses destroyed. What could he do other than surrender? All that remained was the persistent conviction that, in the long run, he was doing the right thing. A conviction that he was afraid to test or examine lest it prove false as well. The silence grew and grew and a great sadness pushed down on Arnie so that he slumped in his chair.

"I do what I have to do," he said, finally, in a voice hoarse with emotion. "I will not return. I have left Israel as I came, voluntarily. You have no hold on me, Gev, no hold. . . ."

General Gev stood up, looking down upon the bowed head. His words were slow in coming and when he did speak, there was the echo of three thousand years of persecution, of death, of mourning, of a great, great sadness.

"You, a Jew, you could do this . . . ?"

There was no possible answer and Arnie remained silent. Gev was soldier enough to see defeat even though he could not understand it. He turned his back, he said nothing more, though what more could be said than this act of turning his back and leaving? He pushed the door open with his fingertips and did not touch it again, to close it or even slam it, but went straight out. Upright, marching, a man who had lost a battle, but who would never lose a war without dying first.

* * *

Ove came in and puttered around the room, stacking the magazines, pulling out a book then putting it back unopened, doing this for some minutes in silence. When he finally spoke it was about something else.

"Listen, what a day it is out. The sun's shining, you can see for miles. You can see the girls' skirts blowing up when they ride their bicycles. I've had enough of this filthy cafeteria food, I'm stuffed solid right up to here with *rug-brod*. I can't face another sandwich. Let's go to Langelinie Pavillonen for lunch. Watch the ships sail by. What do you say?"

There was a stricken look on Arnie's face when he raised his head. He was not a man normally given to strong emotions of any kind, and he had no defenses, no way of dealing with what he now felt. There was the pain—written so clearly on his face that Ove had to turn away and push about the magazines so recently ordered.

"Yes, if you want to. We could have lunch out." His voice was as empty of emotion as his face was lined with it.

They drove in silence down Norre Alle and through the park. It was indeed as Ove had said. The girls were on their high black bikes, flashes of color among the drab jackets of the men, pacing the car on the bicycle paths that bordered the wide street, sweeping in ordered rows across the intersections. Their long legs pumped and their skirts rode up freely and it was a lovely afternoon. Except that Arnie carried with him the memory of a great unhappiness. Ove twisted the little Sprite neatly through the converging traffic at Trianglen and down Osterbrogade to the waterfront. The car shot through a gap in the Langelinie traffic and braked under the rear of the Pavillonen restaurant. They were early enough to get a table at the great glass window that formed one wall. Ove beckoned to the waiter and ordered before they sat down. Even as they were pulling up their chairs a bottle of akvavit appeared, frozen in a block of ice, and a brace of frosted bottles of Tuborg Fine Festival beer.

"Here," Ove said, as the waiter poured out two of the thimble-sized glasses of chilled *snaps*. "Drink this. I'll bet you don't see much of it in Tel-Aviv."

"Skal," they said in ritual unison, and drained the glasses. Arnie sipped at his beer afterward and looked out at the black and white ferry to Sweden, ploughing ponderously by. The buses were pulled up in a waiting row while the tourists clambered over the rocks for a ritual visit to the Little Mermaid, cameras eagerly ready. Beyond them the white sails of

tiny yachts from the basin cut across the cold blue of the Sound. The sea. You could not go more than forty miles from it in Denmark, a seafaring, sea-grit nation if there ever was one. The white triangles of sails were dwarfed by a great liner tied up at Langeliniekaj. Flags and pennants gave her a rakish holiday air, and a sudden burst of steam rose from her front funnel. Moments later the distant moan of her horn could be dimly heard.

"A ship," Arnie said and now, considering his work once again, all trace of what he had been feeling seemed to have vanished. "We need a ship. When we want to try out a larger . . ." He hesitated, and they both looked around with their eyes only, like conspirators, and when he went on it was in a lower voice.

"A larger unit. The first one is too small, a demonstration of theory only. But a big unit will have to be tested on a large scale, to see if we have anything here other than a stupid laboratory demonstration that blows up equipment."

"It will work. I know that it will work."

Arnie twisted his mouth wryly and reached for the bottle.

"Have some more *snaps*," he said.

4

"It is a matter of security," Skou said. He had a first name, Langkilde, but he never mentioned it, perhaps with good reason. "Skou," he insisted, "just call me Skou." As though welcoming all men to the informal friendship of a world-wide billiard parlor. *"Go' davs, Hansen—Go' davs, Jensen—Go' davs, Skou."* But, although he insisted that he was just plain Skou to all men, he was most correct with others.

"We must always take security seriously, Herr Professor Rasmussen," he insisted, his eyes watching everything while he talked. "You have something that requires security, therefore you must have security at all times."

"What we have here . . ."

"Don't tell me, I insist. The fewer who know, the fewer who can tell. Just permit me my security arrangements, and go about your work without a worry."

"Goodness, man, I have no worry. We've only started work recently and no one knows about the project yet."

"Which is the way it should be. I prefer to be in at the beginning or even before the beginning to make my arrangements. If they don't learn one thing they won't learn anything."

He had the knack for constructing pseudo-colloquialisms that made him appear a bit of a fool, which he definitely was not. When he stood, hands stuffed into the pockets of his well-worn tweed jacket, he canted at an angle like a perpetual half-drunk. His blank face and sandy, thinning hair helped this illusion. Ove knew that it was illusion only. Skou had been a police officer for years, his German was perfect, and he had been a rather despised collaborator and card-playing companion of the occupying Germans in Helsingor during the war. He had also been head of the underground in that area, and the angle of his stance had something to do with his being shot by his former drinking companions, then escaping out of a second-story hospital window before they got around to questioning him too closely. Now he was connected with some government bureau, he was never too clear about it, but it added up to security and he got his way whenever he wanted it. He had been in and out of the labs for over a month, enforcing some rules and operations, so what was meant to be private was kept private.

"This all seems very cinematic, Herr Skou," Arnie said. "If we just put the unit in a truck and cover it up no one would ever notice."

"Skou, if you please. The unreal borrows from the real, the cinema from life, if you know what I mean. And maybe we can learn a thing or two from them. It is best to take precautions. A matter of security."

Skou was not to be argued with. They waited, out of sight

inside the Nils Bohr Institute building, while the red and black post office truck pulled up at the loading ramp outside. There was a certain amount of shouting when, backing in, it almost knocked over a stack of milk-bottle crates. But with not too many *"Stop, Hendrik!"* and *"Lidt endnu! Sa er den der!"* cries it put its back doors at the platform edge. Two postmen, bulky in their reddish-pink jackets and heavy with the thud of their wooden-soled *traesko*, brought in some armloads of parcels. That they were more than postmen was apparent by their complete ignoring of the presence of the three watchers: no normal Danish postman could have resisted this opportunity for a chat. Skou silently pointed to the crates that contained the unit and, just as silently, they pushed them into the waiting van. The wide doors were closed, the big padlock sealed, and the truck rumbled its engine and moved out into the road. They watched it until it vanished in the morning traffic.

"Post trucks are not invisible, but they are the next best thing to invisible," Skou said. "They will go to the central office on Kobmagergade, along with many other trucks of the same shape and color. They will emerge a few minutes later—with new numbers, of course—and proceed to the quay. I suggest, gentlemen, that we proceed there as well to greet them upon arrival."

Skou drove them in his car, a disreputable Opel of uncertain age, and did a certain amount of cutting down narrow streets and darting in and out of traffic until he was sure that they were not being followed. He parked near the yacht basin and went to find a telephone while they walked on ahead. A biting wind keened in off the waters of the Oresund, directly from Sweden and the arctic beyond. The sky was low and gray.

"It feels like snow," Ove said.

"Is that the ship?" Arnie asked, looking toward the far end of Langelinie quay, where a single vessel was tied up.

"Yes, the *Isbjorn*. It seemed the best for our needs. After all, we can't be too sure about stress and, old as she is, she's still an icebreaker. I watched her half of last winter keeping the channel clear out here."

Two policemen, massive in their great, long coats, looked out toward Sweden and ignored them when they passed. As did two equally solid men in a car halfway down the quay.

"Skou has his watchdogs out," Ove said.

"I doubt they'll have much to do. In this weather not many sightseers will want to walk along here."

The ship loomed over them, a black wall studded with rows of bulging rivet-heads. The gangplank was down, but no one was in sight on deck. They climbed up slowly, the ramp creaking beneath them.

"Quite an antique," Ove said once they had reached the deck. "But a little too dark to match her 'polar bear' name with all the soot." A thin ribbon of coal smoke rose from her stack from the furnace below.

"Old but strong," Arnie said, pointing at the massive reinforcing in the bows. "The new generation of icebreakers slide up onto the ice and break it with their weight. This old-timer does it the hard way by bashing right on through. This was a wise choice. I wonder where everyone is?"

As though summoned by his words the door to the pilot house swung open and an officer appeared there, as dark and brooding as the ship in his black coat and boots, a great piratical beard concealing the lower part of his face. He stomped over to them and executed a very perfunctory salute.

"I assume that you are the gentlemen I was told to expect. I am Captain Hougaard, the commander of this vessel." There was no warmth at all in his tone or his manner.

They shook hands with him, embarrassed by Skou's instructions not to give their names.

"Thank you for having us aboard, Captain. It was very kind of you to make your ship available," Ove said, trying to be conciliatory.

"I had no choice." He was not in a peacemaking humor. "I was ordered to do so by my superiors. My men are staying below as was also ordered."

"Very kind," Ove said, working hard to keep any sarcastic edge from his words. There was the thin squeal of brakes as the post office truck pulled up on the quay below; a welcome interruption. "Would you be so kind as to have some of your men bring up the packages from that truck?"

Captain Hougaard's only answer was to bellow commands down a hatchway, which brought a half-dozen sailors on the run. They were far more interested than the captain in what was happening, and perhaps grateful for the break in routine.

"Gently with those," Arnie said when they carried the boxes up the gangway. "They can't be dropped or jarred."

"Couldn't treat it more gently if my mother was inside," a blond giant of a seaman said. His wide sideburns vanished into a heroic moustache. He winked at them when the captain wasn't looking.

They had gone over the blueprints of the ship and had selected the engine room as best suited to their needs. The bow end of the space was cut off by a screened wall into a room for the electrician, with his supplies and workbench. The power board and generator were here and, equally important, it was against the outer skin of the ship's hull. The boxes were brought here and, under the watchful eyes of the two physicists, were gently lowered to the deck. When all of the men had gone the captain stepped forward.

"I have been instructed that your work is to be done in absolute privacy. However, since one boiler must be fired, an engineer will have to be stationed out here . . ."

"That's perfectly all right," Arnie broke in.

". . . and when the watch is changed I will change the men myself. I will be in my cabin if you wish to contact me."

"Fine, thank you for the aid, Captain." They watched his retreating back. "I am afraid he doesn't like all this," Arnie said.

"I'm afraid we can't afford to worry about it. Let's get these things uncrated."

Setting up the equipment took most of the day. There were four basic units, electronic equipment of some kind, unidentifiable in their dial-studded black metal cabinets. Heavy cables with multiple-pronged connectors snaked between them, and an even thicker cable ran to the power outlet. While Arnie worried over the connections and adjustment of the equipment, Ove Rasmussen pulled on a pair of cotton workmen's gloves and studied the paint-encrusted, rivet-littered hull of the ship.

"Right here," he said, rapping on a bulging rib with his hammer. He then went to work with steady precision, with hammer and chisel, removing the thick layers of paint that covered the steel. When he had a foot-long area cleaned right down to the bare, shiny metal, he scrubbed it industriously with a wire brush.

"Done," he announced with satisfaction, pulling off the gloves and lighting a cigarette. "Clean as a whistle. Positive contact here and through the entire hull."

"I hope so. This connection is most vital."

A flexible, rectangular-cross-sectioned wave guide protruded from what appeared to be the final unit in the interconnection, and terminated in a complicated bit of brass machining equipped with screw clamps. After a certain amount of filing of metal, and mumbled curses about the intractability of inert matter, they succeeded in fastening it to the prepared section of metal. Arnie made a number of careful settings and switched on the equipment.

"Trickle power," he said. "Just enough to see if we are completing our circuitry."

There was a sudden sharp rapping on the door. Ove went and opened it a crack. Captain Hougaard was outside, looking as annoyed as ever.

"Yes?"

"There is a soldier here who wishes to speak to you." He did not appear to enjoy his rôle as messenger boy.

Ove opened the door just wide enough to slip out through, then carefully closed it behind him. A uniformed sergeant, all web belts, brass clips, high boots, was holding the leather case of a field telephone. The cable from it vanished out of sight up the gangway.

"I was told to bring this to you, sir. The other unit is on the quay outside."

"Thank you, Sergeant. Just put it down here and I'll take care of it."

The door to the electrician's compartment opened and Arnie looked out.

"Could I talk to you, Captain?" he asked.

The captain pointed at the sergeant. "Wait for me on the deck above." He was silent until the man had clumped up the stairway out of earshot. "What is it?"

"We need some skilled help. Perhaps you have someone aboard who can weld—and do a good job? It will take a long time to send ashore for help. This is a matter of national interest," he added when the captain was silent, and appeared reluctant to answer.

"Yes, I'm very much aware of that. The Minister of Trade will have my complete report on this matter. There is Jens; he was a welder in the shipyard. I'll send him down." He went away, the very stomp of his feet radiating annoyance.

Jens turned out to be the moustached giant who had helped bring down the boxes. He appeared, swinging the heavy tanks of a gas welder like toys, smiling innocently.

"Now we get a look at the box of tricks, hey? No secrets from Jens; he sees all and tells nothing. Big mysterious secret affairs, Army, Navy, Marine—even Nils Bohr Institute like Herr Professor Rasmussen here." Both men looked shocked as the big man winked and dropped the pipes and tanks to the deck.

"Perhaps we had better contact—" Arnie said, but was interrupted by Jen's Olympian laugh.

"Don't worry! See all, tell nothing. Jens has been in the Army, in Greenland—in the shipyard, South America. On television I saw the Professor here get the Nobel prize. Gentlemen, don't worry, I am as good a Dane as they come, even if I was born in Jutland, which some lousy Zealanders hold against me, and I even have the Dannebrog tattooed on my chest. Would you like to see it?"

He assumed they would, even before they had a chance to answer, and opened his jacket and shirt to show the white-crossed red flag of Denmark tucked away behind the golden waves of hair.

"That is very good," Arnie said—and shrugged. "I suppose we do not have much choice in the matter. I assume you will not talk about what you see here. . . ."

"If the torturers pulled out every fingernail and toenail on my body I would laugh and spit in their faces without saying a word."

"Yes, I am quite sure that you would. If you will come in here." They stood aside while the big man dragged his equipment in. "It is the hull connection," Arnie told Ove. "Just not good enough. The signal is not getting through. We will have to weld the wave guide to it."

Jens nodded while they explained what must be done, and his welder popped, then hissed to life. He knew his work all right; the captain had not been wrong about that. After removing the wave guide, he brushed the area clean again and scrubbed it with solvent. Only then did he clamp the brass fitting back on and run a true and steady bead down its length, humming cheerfully to himself while he worked.

"Strange looking radios you have here," he said, flashing a brief look at the equipment. "But of course it's not a radio—I know that much, did a bit of radio operating myself in Indonesia. Physics, very complicated stuff."

"Did anyone ever tell you that you talk too much, Jens?" Ove asked.

"Sometimes, but not twice." He closed a scarred fist that looked as big as a soccer ball. Then he laughed. "I talk a lot, but I don't say much. Only to friends." He picked up the equipment and started out. "It has been good speaking with you gentlemen. Don't forget to call on old Jens when you need help." Then he was gone.

"An interesting personality," Arnie said. "Do you think he will tell anyone about this?"

"I hope not. And I doubt it. But I think I'll mention him to Skou, just in case."

"You've caught his security bug."

"Perhaps. But if everything goes according to plan tonight, we are going to have something that we very much want to keep under wraps."

"The signal is fine now," Arnie said, and flipped off the power and leaned back and stretched. "That is all we can do for the moment. What comes next?"

Ove looked at his watch. "Six o'clock and I'm getting hungry. It was arranged for us to eat aboard."

"The captain will really enjoy having us. Boiled fish, boiled potatoes, and alcohol-free beer, I suppose. We should take turns. Why don't you eat first? I am not very hungry."

"After your undoubtedly accurate description neither am I. But I'll volunteer since it was my idea. It will be eleven o'clock before anyone shows up so we have more than enough time."

Arnie puttered with the equipment and worked out an estimate on field strength at maximum output, so the time passed quickly. He unlocked the door when Ove called to him.

"Not one half as bad as we expected. Roast pork and red cabbage, very filling in a hearty, nautical way. Unless you have acquired some dietetic prejudices since I saw you last?"

"Hardly. Modern Judaism is more a state of mind and a cultural heritage than a religion. Though I admit that it is easier to find poultry than pork in Tel-Aviv. I look forward to the dinner."

Just before eleven the field telephone rang with a clanging military urgency. Ove answered it.

"Skou here. The observers are assembling and they wish to know when the demonstration will begin."

"At once, tell them. Tell them I'm on my way up." He rang off and turned to Arnie. "Ready?"

"Ready as we will ever be, I imagine." He took a deep breath. "You had better stay on the other end of this phone so we can be in touch. Keep me informed constantly."

"You know I'll do that. And it's going to work, be sure of that."

"I *hope* that. We will look quite the fools if it does not."

"The laboratory results . . ."

"Are not a field trial. We are going to try that now. Let me know when I am to start."

Ove followed the telephone wire up through the ship and, when he opened the outer door, was pelted in the face by a flurry of fine snow. It was carried by a biting wind that made him close his coat tightly and turn up the collar. From the top of the gangway he could see the huddle of dark figures against the far wall of the quay. Skou was waiting for him when he came down.

"If you are ready they would be pleased if you started. Admiral Sander-Lange there is in his seventies, and we have two generals not much younger."

"The Prime Minister . . .?"

"Decided at the last minute not to come. But there is his representative. The Air Force people are here, everyone on the list."

"We are all ready then. If you bring the phone over, I'll brief them and we can begin."

"I would like some explanation," the admiral said when Ove came up, more than an echo of command still in his old man's voice.

"I'll be happy to, sir. What we hope to do here is to demonstrate the Daleth effect."

"Daleth?" a general asked.

"The fourth letter of the Hebrew alphabet. The symbol that Professor Klein had assigned to the factor in the equation that led to the discovery."

"What discovery?" someone asked, puzzled.

Ove smiled, his features barely visible in the snow-obscured light of the overhead lamp.

"That is what we are here to observe. The Daleth effect has been proven in theory, and in limited laboratory experiments. This is the first time that it has been attempted on a large enough scale to prove whether it will be universally applicable or not. Since there was so much physical difficulty, and security, in setting up this trial, it was decided that observers should be present even if there were a chance of failure."

"Failure of *what*?" an irritated voice asked.

"That will be obvious enough in a few minutes . . ." The telephone rang and Ove broke off. "Yes?"

"Are you ready to start?"

"Yes. Minimum power to begin with?"

"Minimum power. Beginning."

"If you gentlemen will watch the ship," Ove said, covering the mouthpiece.

There was very little to see. Flurries of fine snow swept through the cones of light along the quay. The *Isbjorn*'s gangplank had been raised, as had been instructed, and men stood by on the fore and aft cables, which had been slacked off. The tide had carried the ship away from the quay so that a gap of dark water could be seen. Waves gurgled and slapped between the hull and the stone wall of the quay.

"Nothing yet," Ove said.

"I'm turning up the output."

The men were stamping their feet in the cold and there was an undertone of irritated murmuring. One of them turned to Ove, a complaint ready on his lips, when a sudden high-pitched whining filled the air. It seemed to come from all directions at once, sourceless and irritating, making them feel as though the bones in their skulls were vibrating. This painful aspect of the sound passed quickly, though the vibration itself remained, at a lower pitch, like the string on some celestial bass viol, humming to itself behind the backdrop of the world.

As this first sound died away, a creaking began in the *Isbjorn*, sounding first one part of the hull then the other. There were excited shouts on deck. Something like a shudder passed through the ship and tiny waves broke all around it and sucked at the hull.

"Good Christ, look!" someone gasped. They looked. It was incredible.

As though mounted on a giant underwater piston, the entire mass of the bulky icebreaker was slowly rising in the water. First the Plimsoll line appeared, then the red-leaded bottom of her hull. Dim blots of barnacles spotted it here and there and then, further down, hanks of weed trailed limply. At the stern the lower, barnacled part of the rudder appeared, as well as the propeller, rising steadily until all of its dripping blades were clear of the water. The seamen on shore quickly payed out line as the cables grew taut.

"What is happening? What is this?" one of the observers called out, but his voice was drowned out as others shouted with excitement.

The snow was lessening, blowing away in gaps and swirls;

the lights on the quay now shone clearly on the ship and the sea. Water ran in continuous steams, louder than the slap of waves against the stone.

The keel of the ship was now a good meter above the surface of the Yderhavn channel.

"Arnie, that's it. You've done it!" Ove clutched the phone, looking at the multi-thousand-tonned mass of the ship before him that floated, unsupported, in the air. "It's a meter above the surface at least! Reduce power now, reduce . . ."

"I am." The voice was strained. *"But there is a harmonic building up, a standing wave . . ."*

His words were drowned in a groan of metal from the *Isbjorn* and the ship seemed to shudder. Then, with frightening suddenness, the stern dropped into the water as though some invisible support had been removed, sliding back and down.

The sound was the crash of a giant waterfall, a crescendo of noise. In an instant, rearing up like an attacking animal, a wave of black water surged high over the edge of the quay, hung poised, one meter, two meters above—then plunged. Changing instantly to a bubbling, knee-high foaming tide that tore at the observers and splashed high against the rear wall. It swept the men off their feet, jumbled them together, hurled them apart, left them stranded like beached fish as it drained away in a wide sheet of darkness.

As it subsided the groans and cries went up, and the shouts were echoed aboard the ship.

"Over here, my God, it's the admiral!"

"Don't touch him—that leg's broken at least, maybe worse."

"Get off me . . . !"

"Someone call an ambulance, this man's hurt!"

Heavy boots hammered on the stone as the guards ran up: someone was shouting into a police radio. Aboard the *Isbjorn* there was the clang of metal as she wallowed back and forth, and her captain's voice could be clearly heard above the others.

"Taking water aft—the wooden plugs, you fools—when I get my hands on the people who did this!"

The ear-hurting *bahh-boo* of police ears grew louder, and in the distance there was the rapid clanging of ambulance bells. Headlights raced down the length of the quay as water ran from its edge in a hundred tiny waterfalls.

Ove was dazed, washed against the wall, soaked to the skin and tangled in the wire from the telephone. He pushed himself to a sitting position, back against the rough stone, looking at the frantic scene of shouting men with the *Isbjorn* still rocking in the background. He was shocked by the suddenness of disaster, the wounded, possibly dead men near him. This was terrible; it should not have happened.

At the same time he was filled with such a rising feeling of exultation that he almost shouted aloud. It worked! They had done it! The Daleth effect was as Arnie had predicted it would be.

There was something new in the world, something that had never existed before this night, and from this moment onward the world would never be the same again. He smiled into the darkness, unaware of the blood that was running down his chin, and of the fact that four of his front teeth had been knocked out.

* * *

Snow still drove past spasmodically, first dropping a sheet of obscurity and then lifting it for a tantalizing glimpse. The man on the other side of the channel of the Yderhavn cursed to himself in a continuous guttural monotone. This was the best he could do with such short notice, and it was just not good enough.

He was on the roof of a warehouse, just across the half-mile-wide channel from the Langelinie quay. This area was almost completely deserted after dark, and he had had no trouble avoiding the few night watchmen and police who came by. His glasses were good, the best Zeiss-Ikon 200 mm wide-field night glasses, but they could see nothing if nothing was there. The snow had started soon after the official cars had pulled up on the quay and had been drifting by ever since.

The cars were what had aroused his interest, the high-level

activity so late at night, the concerted motion of a number of military people that he kept under observation. What it meant he had no idea. They had gone to that damned quay, in the dead of night in a snowstorm, to stand and look at a filthy scow of a coal-burning icebreaker. He cursed again and spat into the darkness, an ugly man, uglier now in his anger, with a tight mouth, round head, bullet neck, and thin gray hair cropped so short it might have been shaved.

What were these thick and stupid Danes up to? Something had happened; there had been an accident docking the ship perhaps, men had been knocked down. There had been a disturbance in the water. But there had been no sound of an explosion. Now there was plenty of excitement, ambulances and police cars coming from all sides. Whatever had happened had happened; there would be nothing else of importance to be seen here tonight. He cursed again as he rose, chilled, his knees stiff and cracking with the effort.

Something had happened, that was certain. And he was damned well going to find out what it was. That was what he was paid to do and that was what he enjoyed doing.

The ambulances clanged away, and it would have taken a keen eye in the darkness to see that the icebreaker now rode lower in the water.

5

"Not much of a view," Bob Baxter admitted, "but it's one that I find inspiring in a way. It's kind of hard for me to forget my job when I look out of this window."

Baxter was a thin, gangling man who seemed to fold at the joints like a carpenter's rule. His face was bland, instantly forgettable, and its most memorable feature was the thick, black-framed glasses that he wore. Without them you might not recognize him. Which was perhaps why he wore them.

He slumped when he sat, deep in the swivel chair behind the desk, pointing out of the window with a freshly sharpened, yellow HB pencil stamped PROPERTY OF THE U.S. GOVERNMENT.

The only other man in the small office sat, bolt upright, on the front half of his chair and nodded stiffly. This was not the first time he had heard about the view. He was a solid, ugly man with tight-clamped lips and a very round head only partially covered with a stubble of gray hair. The name he was known by was Horst Schmidt, which is just as much a hotel register name as is John Smith.

"Peaceful in a way," Baxter said, jabbing the point of the pencil at the white stones and green trees. "Nothing more peaceful than a graveyard I guess. And do you know what that building with the fancy roof is, right on the other side of the graveyard?"

"The Embassy of the Union of Soviet Socialist Republics." His English was accented but good, with a marked tendency to roll the Rs deep in the throat.

"Pretty symbolic that." Baxter swung about and dropped the pencil back onto his desk. "The American embassy being right across this graveyard from the Russian embassy. Gives you something to think about. What have you found out about that trouble the other night down by the waterfront?"

"It has not been easy, Mr. Baxter. Everyone is being very close-mouthed." Schmidt reached into the inner pocket of his jacket and withdrew a folded sheet of paper, holding it at arm's length and squinting to read it. "This is the list of the people hospitalized with injuries, all of them admitted at roughly the same time. They are—"

"I'll make a xerox of that list so you can skip the details. Can you just give me a summary now?"

"Of course. One admiral, one major general, one colonel, one other rank, one high-ranking member of the Ministry of State. Five individuals in all. I have good reason to believe that an unidentified number of other individuals were treated for bruises and dismissed. Among these numbered members of the Air Force."

"Very good. Most efficient."

"It was not easy. Military hospital records are hard to come by. There were expenses. . . ."

"Just submit your gyp sheet. You'll be paid, no fear. Now the sixty-four-dollar question, if I may say so myself, is what *caused* all these injuries?"

"That is difficult to determine, you must realize. There is a ship involved, the *Isbjorn*, an icebreaker."

"That is not what I would call startling news, since we have known it since the first day." Baxter frowned slightly and pushed the handful of sharpened pencils into a neat row on the unmarked green blotter before him. The only other item on the desk was a folding, leather-type plastic frame containing the picture of a round-faced, smiling woman holding two equally moon-faced, but surly, children. "There must be more."

"There is, sir. The *Isbjorn* has been towed across to the Naval shipyard in Christianshavn where it is being repaired. It appears to have suffered some sort of hull damage, possibly through collision. I have been able to determine that whatever is responsible for the damage to the ship also injured the men. Getting this bit of information alone has been immensely difficult because of the security curtain that has been clamped down on the entire affair. This is enough to lead me to believe that something very important is going on."

"I believe the same thing, Horst, the same thing." Baxter's eyes unfocused in thought and his fingers touched one of the pencils, picked it up, carried it to his mouth where he gnawed lightly at it. "This appears to be a *big* thing for the Danes, all the military involved, their state department, even a damned icebreaker. And that icebreaker makes me think of ice and ice makes me think of Russia and I would like to know just what the hell is going on."

"You haven't then . . ." Horst smiled a completely unhumorous grin that revealed a badly matched collection of yellow teeth, steel teeth, even the unexpected luxury of a gold tooth. "That is, I mean, there should be some information through NATO, should there not?"

"Which is none of your damn business whether there is or not." Baxter frowned at the dented, spit-damp end of the pencil, then threw it into the wastebasket. "You are here to supply information to me, not the other way around. Though you might as well know that officially nothing has ever happened and no one is going to say one damned word to us about it." Under the cover of the desk he wiped his damp fingertips on his pants leg.

"That is very disloyal of them," Horst said with complete lack of emotion. "After all that your country has done for them."

"You can say that again." Baxter glanced quickly at his wrist watch. It was gold and contained an extraordinary number of hands and buttons. "You can give me a report in a week. Same day, same time. You should be able to find out something more by then."

Schmidt passed over the piece of paper with the names.

"You said that you wished to photocopy this. And then there is the matter of . . ." He had his hand out, palm up, and he smiled quickly before lowering it.

"Money. Come right out and say it, Horst. Money. Nothing to be ashamed of. We all work for money, that's what keeps the wheels turning. I'll be right back."

Baxter took the paper and went through the connecting door to the next office. Schmidt sat, unmoving, while he waited, showing no interest in the desk or the filing cabinet against the wall. He yawned once, widely, then belched, smacking his lips afterward with a dissatisfied expression. He took two white tablets from a plastic box in his pocket and chewed on them. Baxter returned and gave him back the sheet of paper and a long, unmarked envelope. Schmidt slipped them both into his pocket.

"Aren't you going to count it?" asked Baxter.

"You are a man of honor." He stood up, every inch the middle-class middle-European in his wide-lapeled dark blue suit, heavy black shoes, wide-cut trousers with cuffs big enough to swallow his feet. Baxter's eyebrows raised up, above the black frames of his glasses, but he said nothing. Schmidt took his coat and scarf from the stand in the corner, both as dark and coarse of texture as the wide-brimmed hat. He left without another word, using the door that opened into the gray and featureless hall. There was no nameplate on the outside of the door, just the number 117. Instead of turning into the lobby, he continued along the hallway, then down a flight of stairs to the United States Information Service Library. There, without looking at the titles, he took two books from the shelf nearest the door. While they were being checked out he shrugged into his coat. When he emerged into Osterbrogade a few minutes later he walked close behind another man who was also carrying books. The other turned right, but he turned left, and walked stolidly past Garnisons churchyard and on to the Osterport subway station.

Inside the station he made use of almost all of the facilities, one after another. He bought a newspaper at the kiosk by the entrance, turning about and looking over the top of it to see who came in after him. He went to the toilet at the far end. He checked the books and the newspaper into an automat locker and pocketed the key. He went down one staircase to the trains and, although it was against the law to cross the tracks, managed to come up some time later by way of a different staircase. This appeared to be thirsty work and he finally had a glass of draft Carlsberg from the luncheonette, standing up and drinking it at one of the chest-high tables. All of these actions appeared to have accomplished what they had been designed to do because, after wiping the foam from his lips with the back of his hand, he emerged from the rear entrance of the station and walked briskly down Ostbanegade, next to the tracks where they emerged from the tunnel into the watery winter sunshine. At the first corner he turned left and walked down along the other side of the churchyard. He was alone in the street.

When he was positive of this he turned about smartly and walked through the open, high wrought-iron gates and into the Soviet embassy.

6

THE BALTIC

"Ja, Ja," Captain Nils Hansen said into the telephone, *"jeg skal nok tale med hende. Tak for det."* He sat, tapping his fingers against the phone while he waited. The man who had identified himself only as Skou stood looking out of the window at the gray, wintry afternoon. There was the distant banshee scream of jets as one of the big planes taxied in from the runway.

"Hello, Martha," Nils continued in English. "How is everything? Fine. No. I'm at Kastrup, just set down a little while ago. A nice tall wind out of Athens, brought us in early. And that's the trouble, I'm going right out again. . . ." He nodded agreement with the voice that rustled in his ear, looking more than a little unhappy.

"Listen, darling, you are completely correct and I couldn't agree more—but there is absolutely nothing we can do about it. The powers that be have willed otherwise. I can't fly, too many hours, but they can fly me. One of the pilots—a Swede, what else?—is down with appendicitis in Calcutta. I'm going out on the next flight, in fact they are holding it for me right now, and I'll sleep and get another night's sleep at the Oberoi Grand, so I'll be able to take his flight out tomorrow. Right. . . . Nearer forty-eight hours I would say. I am as sorry to miss the dinner as you are and please tell the Overgaards that I am crying because I shall miss her *dyresteg* and instead of fine Scandinavian venison I shall be eating gut-rotting curries and will suffer for a week. Of course, *skat*, I'll miss you too and I'll make them pay me a bonus and I'll buy you something nice with it. Yes . . . okay . . . good-bye."

Nils hung up and looked with open dislike at Skou's turned back. "I don't enjoy lying to my wife," he said.

"I'm very sorry, Captain Hansen, but it cannot be

avoided. A matter of security, you know. Take precautions today and tomorrow takes care of itself." He looked at his watch. "The Calcutta plane is just leaving, and you are listed as being aboard. You are registered at the Calcutta hotel, though you will not be able to receive phone calls. Everything has been arranged with the utmost detail. The ruse is a necessary but harmless one."

"Necessary for *what*? You appear out of nowhere, take me to this office, show me letters with big names on them requesting my service, including one from my commander in the Air Force Reserve, extract my promise to cooperate, induce me to lie to my wife—but really tell me nothing. What the devil is going on?"

Skou nodded seriously, looked around the room as if it were lined with countless eavesdropping bugs, and did everything but put his finger to his lips: he radiated secrecy.

"If I could tell you I would. I cannot. Within a very short time you will know all about it. Now—can we leave? I'll take your bag."

Nils grabbed it up before the other could touch it and stood, jamming his uniform cap onto his head. He was six feet four inches tall in stockinged feet: now, in uniform, cap, and belted raincoat, he loomed large enough to fill the small room. Skou opened the door and Nils stamped out after him. They exited through the back door of the operations building where a cab was waiting for them, a Mercedes diesel hammering and throbbing while its engine idled. As soon as they had entered the driver put down his flag and started, without instructions. When they left the airport they turned right, away from Kastrup.

"That's interesting," Nils said, looking out of the window, the scowl now vanished from his face. He could never stay angry very long. "Instead of going to Kobenhavn, and the exciting world beyond, we head south on this little pool table of a potato-growing island. What can we possibly find of interest in this direction?"

Skou reached over into the front seat and took up a black topcoat and a dark beret. "Would you be so kind as to take off your uniform coat and cap and put these on. I am sure that your trousers will not be identified with an SAS uniform."

"Cloak and dagger, by God," Nils said, struggling out of his coat in the cramped back seat. "I suppose this good and honest cab driver is in on the whole thing?"

"Of course."

The capacious front seat now yielded up a small suitcase just large enough for the discarded coat and cap. Nils pulled the collar of his new coat up, pulled the beret down over his eyes and buried his big chin in the collar.

"There, do I look conspiratorial enough now?" He could not stop himself from grinning. Skou did not share his humor.

"I'll ask you, please, not to do anything that will draw attention to us. This is a very important matter, I can tell you that much."

"I'm sure of it."

They rode in silence after that, through a drab landscape of freshly plowed fields waiting for the spring sowing. It was a short drive to the fishing village of Dragor, and Nils looked suspiciously at the old red-brick buildings as they passed. They did not stop, but continued on to the harbor.

"Sweden?" Nils asked. "Aboard the car ferry?"

Skou did not trouble himself to answer, and they drove right by the ferry slip to the small harbor. A few pleasure craft were tied up here, including a fair-sized inboard launch.

"If you will follow me, please," Skou said, and grabbed Nils's bag before he could get it himself. He led the way out on the dock, carrying both bags. Nils followed meekly after, wondering just what the hell he was getting into. Skou climbed aboard the launch and put the bags into the cabin, then waved Nils aboard. The man at the wheel appeared to ignore all this, but he did start the engine.

"I'll say good-bye, then," Skou said. "I think it will be most comfortable traveling in the cabin."

"Traveling where?"

Skou left without answering and began to untie the mooring lines. Nils shrugged, then bent over to get through the low cabin door. He dropped onto the bench inside and discovered, tardily because of the dim light that filtered through the small portholes, that he was not alone.

"Good afternoon," he said to the muffled figure on the far end of the other bench, and received a noncommittal answer in return. As his eyes adjusted to the light, he realized that there was a suitcase at the other man's feet and that he was wearing a black coat and dark beret.

"How about that," Nils laughed. "Looks like they caught you too. We're wearing the same uniform."

"I don't know what you are talking about," the other said testily, pulling off the beret and jamming it into his pocket. Nils moved along the bench to sit opposite him.

"Oh yes you do. That Skou with his mysterious ways. Very little imagination though when it comes to disguise. I'll bet you were drafted for a secret job in a big hurry and rushed over here."

"How do you know that?" the other asked, sitting up.

"Instinct." Nils pulled off his beret and pointed to it—then looked closer at the other man's face. "Don't I know you from somewhere? A party or something—no, from the magazine. You're the submarine fellow who helped salvage that Seven-oh-Seven off the coast. Carlsson, Henriksen or something. . . ."

"Henning Wilhelmsen."

"Nils Hansen."

They shook hands automatically after this exchange of names, and the air of tension lessened. It was warm in the tiny cabin and Nils opened his coat. The motor chugged steadily as they pulled away from shore. Wilhelmsen looked at the other's uniform.

"Now isn't that interesting," he said. "A naval commander and an SAS pilot wallowing out into the Oresund aboard a scow. What could this possibly mean?"

"Maybe Denmark has an aircraft carrier we don't know about?"

"Then why me? It would have to be a submarine aircraft carrier, and *that* I would have heard something about. How about a drink?"

"The bar isn't open."

"It is now." Wilhelmsen pulled a leather-covered flask

from his side pocket. "The motto of the submarine service is 'Be prepared.' "

Nils smacked his lips unconsciously as dark liquid was poured into the metal cup. "I can't if I'm going to fly in the next twelve hours."

"Little chance of that out here, unless this barge sprouts wings. Besides, this is navy rum, alcohol free."

"I accept your offer."

The rum tasted quite good and put a better temper to the afternoon. After a certain amount of circling around the topic they exchanged information, only to discover this merely doubled their lack of knowledge. They were going somewhere for reasons unknown. After squinting at the setting sun they agreed that the only bit of Danish landscape that lay in this direction was the island of Bornholm, which was an impossibility in their light craft. A half-hour later their question was answered when the launch's engine was cut and the portholes on the starboard side suddenly darkened.

"A ship, of course," Henning Wilhelmsen said, and poked his head out of the door. "The *Vitus Bering*."

"Never heard of her."

"I certainly have. It's a Marine Institute ship. I was aboard her last year when she was mother ship for ***Blaeksprutten***, the small experimental sub. I did the trial runs."

Feet thudded to the deck and a sailor poked his head in and asked for their baggage. They passed it out, then followed him up the heaving ladder. A ship's officer invited them to the wardroom, then showed them the way. There were more than a dozen uniformed men waiting there, representatives of all the armed forces, as well as four civilians. Nils recognized two of them, a politician he had once had as a passenger, and Professor Rasmussen, the Nobel prize winner.

"If you will sit down, gentlemen," Ove Rasmussen said, "I'll tell you why we are all here."

* * *

By dawn the next morning they were far out in the Baltic, in international waters, a hundred miles from land. Arnie had slept badly; he wasn't much of a sailor and the pitching of the ship had kept him awake. He was the last one on deck, and he joined the others as they watched *Blaeksprutten* being swung up out of the hold.

"Looks like a toy," Nils Hensen said. The big pilot, although he wore his SAS cap was, like all of the others, now dressed in high rubber boots, sweaters, and heavy wool pants to stop the cutting arctic wind. It was a lowering winter day with the clouds pressing down and the horizon close by.

"She's no toy—and she's bigger than she looks," Wilhelmsen defended warmly. "With a crew of three she can still carry a couple of observers. Dives well, good control, plenty of depth . . ."

"No propellers though," Nils said gloomily, winking at the other. "They must have got broken off . . ."

"This is a sub, not one of your flying machines! It has water impellers, jets, just like those stupid great things of yours. That's why it's called *Blaeksprutten*—it moves by jetting water just like a squid."

Arnie caught Ove's eye and motioned him aside.

"A perfect day for the trials," Ove said, pushing at his new front teeth with his tongue; they still felt strange. "The visibility is down and nothing at all on the radar. An Air Force plane overflew us earlier and reported the nearest ship to be over a hundred and forty kilometers distant. Just a Polish coastal freighter at that."

"I would like to be aboard for the tests, Ove."

Ove took him lightly by the shoulder. "Don't think I don't know that. I don't want to take your place. But the Minister thinks that you are too valuable a man to be risked this first time out. And I guess that he is right. But I would still change if I could—only they won't let me. The admiral knows the order and he'll see that it is obeyed. Don't worry—I'll take good care of your baby. We've eliminated that harmonic trouble and there's nothing else that can go wrong. You'll see."

Arnie shrugged with submission, knowing that further argument would be useless.

With much waving and shouted instructions the small sub

was swung out and lowered into the sea. Henning Wilhelmsen was down the ladder almost before it touched, leaping aboard. He vanished down the hatch on top of the conning tower, and a few minutes later there was an underwater rumbling as her engines started. Henning popped up through the hatch and waved. "Come aboard," he called out.

Ove took Arnie's hand. "It's going to be all right," he said. "Since we installed the Daleth unit, we have checked it over a dozen different times."

"I know, Ove. Good luck."

Ove climbed down the ladder with Nils Han en right behind him. They entered and closed the hatch.

"Cast off," Henning said, his voice booming from the loudspeaker that, connected to the short-range, low-powered radio, had been installed on deck. The lines were pulled free and the little sub turned and began to move away. Arnie took up the microphone and pressed to talk.

"Take it out about three hundred meters before beginning the test."

"Ja vel!"

The ship's engines had been stopped, and the *Vitus Bering* rolled in the easy sea. Arnie held tight to the railing and watched the sub move away. His face was as composed as always, but he could feel his heartbeat, faster then he ever remembered. Theory is one thing, practice another. As Skou might say. He smiled to himself. This was the final test.

There were field glasses around his neck and he fumbled them to his eyes as the sub turned and began to circle the mother ship in a wide circle. Through the glasses the craft was very clear, moving steadily, its hull barely awash as the waves broke against it.

Then—yes, it was true—the waves were splashing against the side and more of the hull was visible. It appeared to be rising higher and higher in the water, floating unnaturally high—then rising even further.

Until, like a great balloon, it rested on the surface.

Rose above the surface. Went up gracefully five, ten, thirty meters. Arnie dropped the glasses on their strap and held the rail tightly, looking, frozen.

With all the grace of a lighter-than-air craft, the twenty-ton, thick-hulled submarine was floating a good forty meters above the sea. Then it seemed to rotate on some invisible bearing until it pointed directly at the mother ship. Moving slowly it drifted their way, sliding over their upturned faces, a spray of fine droplets falling from its still dripping hull. No one spoke—struck speechless by the almost unbelievable sight—and the stuttering of the submarine's diesel engines could be clearly heard. Without turning his eyes away, Arnie groped for the microphone and switched it on.

"You can bring it in now. I think that we can call the experiment a success."

7

With the blackboard behind him and the circle of seated, eager listeners before him, Arnie felt very much at home. As though he were back in a classroom at the university, not the wardroom of the *Vitus Bering*. He resisted the impulse to turn and write his name, ARNIE KLEIN, in large letters upon the board. But he did write DALETH EFFECT very clearly at the top, then the Hebrew letter ד after it.

"If you will be patient for a moment, I must give you a small amount of history in order to explain what you witnessed this morning. You will remember that Israel conducted a series of atmospheric research experiments with rockets a few years ago. The tests served a number of functions, not the least of which was to show the surrounding Arab countries that we . . . that is they, Israel . . . had home-manufactured rockets and did not depend upon the vagaries of foreign supplies. Due to the physical limitations imposed by the surrounding countries, and the size of Israel, there was very little choice of trajectories. Straight up and straight back down was all that we could do, and some very exacting control techniques had to be worked out to accomplish this. But a rocket that rose vertically and stayed directly above the launch site on the ground proved an invaluable research device for a number of disciplines. A trailing smoke cloud supplied the meteorologists with wind direction and speed at all altitudes, while internal instrumentation recordings later coordinated this with atmospheric pressure and temperature. Once out of the atmosphere there were even more experiments, but the one that we concern ourselves with now is the one that inadvertently revealed what can only be called gravimetric anomalies." He started to write the word on the blackboard, but controlled himself at the last moment.

"My interest at this time was in quasars, and the possible source of their incomprehensible energies. Even the total annihilation of matter, as you know, cannot explain the energy generation of quasars. But this became almost incidental because—completely by chance—this rocket probe was out of the atmosphere when a solar flare started. It was there for almost fifty minutes. Other probes, in the past, have been launched as soon as a flare has been detected, but this means a lag of an hour at least after the original explosion of energy. Therefore I had the first readings to work with on the complete buildup of a solar flare. Magnetometer, cosmic ray particles—and something that looked completely irrelevant at the time: the engineering data. This drew my attention because I had been working for some years on certain aspects of the Einsteinian quantum theory that relate to gravity. This research had just proven to be a complete dead end, but it was still on my mind. So when the others discarded some of the data because they believed the telemetry was misreading due to the strong magnetic fields, I investigated in greater detail. The data was actually sound, but it showed that a wholly inexplicable force was operating that seemingly reduced the probe's weight, but not its mass. That is to say that its gravitational mass and inertial mass were temporarily unequal. I assigned the symbol *Daleth* to this discrepancy factor and then sought to find out what it was. To begin with, I at once thought of the Schwarzchild mass, or rather the application of this to the four-dimensional continuum of the Minkowski universe. . . .''

The baffled expressions on all the faces finally drew Arnie's attention—including one high-ranking officer whose eyes were glazed, almost bulging—and he slowed and stopped. He coughed into his fist to cover his confusion. These were not physics students after all. Turning to the board he added another underscore to the *Daleth*.

"Not to go into too many details, I will attempt to explain this observation in simple language. Though you must understand that this is an approximation only of what occurred. I had something that I could not explain, though it was something that was obviously there. Like taking a dozen chicken eggs and hatching them and having an eagle come out of one. It is there, clearly enough, but why and how we do not know."

A relieved chuckle moved across the wardroom, and there were even a few smiles as they finally found themselves understanding something that was being said. Encouraged, Arnie stayed on common ground.

"I began to work with the anomaly, first setting up mathematical models to determine its nature, then some simple experiments. In physics, as in all things, knowing just what you are looking for can be a great aid. For example, it is easier to find a criminal in a city if you have a description or a name. Once helium had been detected in the spectrum of the sun its presence was uncovered here on Earth. It had been here all the time, unnoticed until we knew what to look for. The same is true of the Daleth effect. I knew what to look for and I found answers to my questions. I speculated that it might be possible to control this . . ." He groped for a word. "It is not true, and I should not do it, but for the moment let us call it an 'energy'. Remembering all the time that it is *not* an energy. I set up an experiment in an attempt to control this energy which had rather spectacular results. Control was possible. Once tapped, the Daleth energy could be modulated; this was little more than an application of current technology. You saw the results this morning when *Blaeksprutten* rose into the air. This was a very limited demonstration. There is no reason why the submarine could not have traveled above the atmosphere at speeds of our own choosing."

A hand was raised, with positive assurance, and Arnie nodded in that direction. At least someone was listening closely enough to want to ask a question. It was an Air Force officer, looking young for the high rank that he held.

"You'll pardon my saying this, Professor Klein, but aren't you getting something for nothing? Which I have been taught is impossible. You are negating the Newtonian laws of motion. There is not enough power in the sub's engines, no matter how applied, other than by a block and tackle, to lift its mass and hold it suspended. You mentioned relativity, which is based solidly on the conservation of momentum, mass energy, and electric charge. What appears to have happened here must throw at least two out of the three into doubt."

"Very true," Arnie agreed. "But we are not ignoring these restrictions; we are simply using a different frame of reference in which they do not apply. As an analogy I ask you to consider the act of turning a valve. A few foot pounds will open a valve that will allow compressed gas to leave a tank and expand into a bag and cause a balloon to rise. An even better comparison might be to think of yourself as hanging by a cord from that bag, high above the Earth. An ounce or so of pressure on a sharp blade will cut the cord and bring you back to the ground with highly dramatic effects."

"But cutting the cord just releases the kinetic energy stored by lifting me to that height," the officer said warmly. "It is the gravity of the Earth that brings me down."

"Precisely. And it was the released gravity of Earth that permitted *Blaeksprutten* to fly."

"But that is impossible!"

"Impossible or not, it happened," an even higher ranking Air Force officer called. "You damned well better believe your own eyes, Preben, or I'll have you grounded."

The officer sat down, scowling at the general laughter, which died away as Admiral Sander-Lange began to speak.

"I believe everything you say about the theory of your machine, Professor Klein, and I thank you for attempting to explain it to us. But I hope you will not be insulted when I say that, at least for me, it is not of the utmost importance. Many years back I stopped trying to understand all the boxes of tricks they were putting on my ships and set myself the task of only understanding what they did and how they could be used. Could you explain the possibilities, the things that might be accomplished by application of your Daleth effect?"

"Yes, of course. But I hope that you will understand that there are still a number of 'ifs' attached. If the effect can be applied as we hope—and the next experiment with *Blaeksprutten* will determine that—and if the energy demands are within reason to obtain the desired results, then we will have what might be called a true space drive."

"What exactly do you mean by that?" Sander-Lange asked.

"First consider the space drive we now use, reaction rockets such as the ones that power the Soviet capsule that is now on its way to the Moon. Rockets move through application of the law of action-and-reaction. Throw something away in one direction and you move in the other. Thousands of pounds of fuel, reaction mass, must be lifted for every pound that arrives at its destination. This process is expensive, complicated, and of only limited usage. A true space drive, independent of this mass-to-load ratio, would be as functionally practical as an automobile or a seagoing ship. It would power a true spacegoing ship. The planets might become as accessible as the other parts of our own world. Since reaction mass is not to be considered, a true space drive could be run constantly, building up acceleration to midpoint in its flight, then reversing direction and decelerating continuously until it landed. This would make a simply incredible difference in the time needed to fly to the Moon or the planets."

"How big a difference?" someone asked. "Could you give us some specific figures?"

Arnie hesitated, thinking, but Ove Rasmussen stood to answer. "I think I can give you some help. I have been working it out while we have been talking." He lifted his slide rule and made a few rapid calculations. "If we have a continuous acceleration and deceleration of one G—one gravity—there will be no feeling of either free fall or excess weight to passengers in the vehicle. This will be an acceleration of . . . nine hundred eighty—we'll call it a thousand for for simplicity—centimeters per second per second. The Moon is, on the average, about four hundred thousand kilometers distant. The result would therefore be . . ."

There was complete silence as he made the calculations. He read off the result, frowned, then did it over again. The answer appeared to be the same, because he looked up and smiled.

"If the Daleth effect does produce a true space drive, there is something new under the sun, gentlemen.

"We will be able to fly from here to the Moon in a little under four hours."

During the unbelieving silence that followed he made another calculation.

"The voyage to Mars will take a bit longer. After all, the red planet is over eighty million kilometers distant at its closest conjunction. But even that voyage will be made in about thirty-nine hours. A day and three-quarters. Not very long at all."

* * *

They were stunned. But as they thought of the possibilities opened up by the Daleth effect a babble of conversation rose, so loud that Arnie had to tap on the blackboard with his chalk to get their attention and to silence them. They listened now with a fierce attention. "As you see, the possibilities of the exploitation of the Daleth drive are almost incalculable. We must change all of our attitudes about the size of the solar system. But before we sail off to the Moon for a weekend of exploration we must be sure that we have an adequate source of motive power. Will the drive work away from the Earth's surface? Is it precisely controllable—that is can we make the minute course adjustments needed to reach an object of astronomical distances? Do we have a power source great enough to supply the energy demands for the voyage? Is the drive continuously reliable?

"The next flight of *Blaekspruttten* should answer most of these questions. The craft will attempt to rise to the top of the Earth's atmosphere.

"As the most qualified person in regard to the drive equipment, I shall personally conduct the tests." He looked around, jaw clamped, as though expecting to be differed with, but there was only silence. This was his day.

"Thank you. I would suggest then that the second trial be begun immediately."

8

"I'm beginning to see why they might need an airline pilot aboard a submarine," Nils said, spinning the wheel that sealed the lower hatch in the conning tower.

"Keep the log, will you?" Henning asked, pointing to the open book on the little navigator's table fixed to the bulkhead.

"I'll do just that," Nils said, looking at his watch and making an entry. "If this thing works you'll be the only sub commander ever to get flight pay."

"Take us out, please, will you, Commander Wilhelmsen?" Arnie said, intent upon his instruments. "At least as far as you did the first time."

"Ja vel." Henning advanced the impeller one notch and the pumps throbbed beneath their feet. He sat in the pilot's seat just ahead of the conning tower. The hull rose here in a protuberance that contained three round, immensely thick ports. A control wheel, very much like that in an airplane, determined direction. For turning left and right it varied the relative speed of the twin water jets that propelled the sub. Tail planes aft caused them to rise or fall.

"Two hundred meters out," Henning announced, and eased off on the power.

"The pumps for your jets, are they mechanical?" Arnie asked.

"Yes, electrically driven."

"Can you cut them off completely and still maintain a constant output from your generator? We have voltage regulators, but it would help if you could produce as constant a supply as is possible."

Henning threw a series of switches. "All motor power off. There is still an instrumentation drain as well as the atmosphere equipment. I can cut them off—for a limited time—if you like?"

"No, this will be fine. I am now activating the drive unit and will rise under minimum power to a height of approximately one hundred meters."

Nils made an entry in the log and looked at the waves splashing at the porthole nearest him. "You don't happen to have an altimeter fitted aboard this tub, do you, Henning?"

"Not really."

"Pity. Have to get one installed. And radar instead of that sonar. I have a feeling that you're getting out of your depth . . ."

Henning had a pained look and shook his head dolefully—then glanced at the port as a vibration, more felt than heard, swept through the sub. The surface of the water was dropping at a steady rate.

"Airborne now," he said, and looked helplessly at his useless instruments. The ascent continued; moments passed.

"One hundred meters," Nils said, estimating their height above the ship below. Arnie made a slight adjustment and turned to face them.

"There appears to be more than enough power in reserve even while the drive is holding the mass of this submarine at this altitude. The equipment is functioning well and is in no danger of overloading. Are you gentlemen ready?"

"I'm never going to be more ready."

"Push the button or whatever, Professor. Just hanging here seems to be doing me no good."

The humming increased and their chairs pressed up against them. Nils and Henning stared through the ports, struck silent by emotion, as the tiny submarine leapt toward the sky. A thin whistle vibrated through the hull as the air rushed past outside, scarcely louder than the sigh of the air-conditioning unit. The engine throbbed steadily. Seemingly without effort, as silently as a film taken from an ascending rocket, their strange craft was hurling itself into the sky. The sea below seemed to smooth out, their mother ship shrinking to the size of a model, then to a bathtub toy, before the low-lying clouds closed in around them.

"This is worse than flying blind," Nils said, his great hands clenching and unclenching. "Seat of the pants, not a single instrument other than a compass, it's just not right."

Arnie was the calmest of the three, too attentive to his instruments to even take a quick glimpse through one of the ports. "The next flight will have all the instrumentation," he said. "This is a trial. Just up and down like an elevator. Meanwhile the Daleth unit shows that we are still vertical in relation to the Earth's gravity, still moving away from it at the same speed."

The cloud layers were thick, but soon fell away beneath their keel. Then the steady rhythm of the diesel engines changed just as Arnie said, "The current—it is dropping! What is wrong?"

Henning was in the tiny engine compartment, shouting out at them.

"Something, the fuel, I don't know, they're losing power . . ."

"The atmospheric pressure." Nils said. "We've reached our ceiling. The oxygen content of the air is way down!"

The engine coughed, stuttered, almost died, and a shudder went through the submarine. An instant later they started to fall.

"Can't you do something?" Arnie called out, working desperately at the controls. "The flow—so erratic—the Daleth effect is becoming inoperable. Can't you stabilize the current?"

"The batteries!" Henning dived for his position as he

spoke, almost floating in the air, so quickly was their fall accelerating.

He clutched at the back of his chair, missed, floated up and hit painfully against the periscope housing and bounced back. This time his fingers caught the chair and he pulled himself down into it and strapped in. He reached for the switches.

"Current on—full!"

The fall continued. Arnie glanced quickly at the other two men.

"Get ready. I have cut the drive completely. When I engage it now I am afraid that the reaction will not be gentle because—"

Metal screeched, equipment crashed and broke, and there were hoarse gasps as the sudden deceleration drove the air from their lungs. They were slammed down hard into their chairs, painfully, and for an instant they hovered at the edge of blackout as the blood drained from their brains.

Then it was over and they were gasping for air, dizzily. Henning's face was a white mask streaked with red, bleeding from an unnoticed scalp wound where his skull had struck the periscope. Outside there were only clouds. The engine ran smoothly and the air hushed from the vents, soft background to their rough breathing.

"Let us not—" Nils said, taking a deep breath. "Let us not . . . do *that* again!"

"We are maintaining altitude with no lateral motion," Arnie said, his words calm despite the hardness of his breathing. "Do you wish to return—or to complete the test?"

"As long as this doesn't happen again, I'm for going on," Nils said.

"Agreed. But I suggest that we operate on the batteries."

"How is the charge?"

"Excellent. Down less than five percent."

"We will go back up. Let me know when the charge is down to seventy percent and we will return. That should give us an acceptable safety margin. Plus the fact that engines can be restarted when we are low enough."

It was smooth, exhilarating. The clouds dropped below

them and the engine labored. Henning shut it down and sealed the air intake. They rose.

"Five thousand meters high at least," Nils said, squinting at the cloud cover below with a pilot's eye. "Most of the atmosphere is below us now."

"Then I can step up the acceleration. Please note the time."

"It's all in the log. Some of it in a very shaky handwriting, I can tell you."

The curvature of the Earth was visible, the atmosphere a blue band above it tapering into the black of space. The brighter stars could be seen; the sun burned like a beacon and, shining through the port, threw a patch of eye-hurting brightness onto the deck. The upward pressure ceased.

"Here we are," Arnie said. "The equipment is functioning well, we are holding our position. Can anyone estimate our altitude?"

"One hundred fifty kilometers," Nils said. "Ninety or a hundred miles. It looks very much like the pictures shot from the satellites at that altitude."

"Battery reserve seventy-five percent and dropping slowly."

"Yes, it takes power to hover, scarcely less than for acceleration."

"Then we've done it!" Nils said and, even louder when the enormity struck him, "We've done it! We can go anywhere—do anything. We've really done it . . ."

"Battery reserve nearing seventy percent."

"We will go down then."

"A little slower than last time?"

"You can be sure of that."

More gently than a falling leaf, the submarine dropped. They passed through a silvery layer of high cirrus clouds.

"Won't we be coming down much further to the west?" Nils asked. "The Earth will have rotated out from under us so we won't be able to set down in the same spot."

"No, I have compensated for that motion. We should be no more than a mile or two from the original position."

"Then I had better get on the radio." Henning switched it on. "We'll be in range soon, and we'll want to tell them . . ."

A voice came clearly through the background static, speaking the fast, slang-filled Copenhagen Danish that only a native of that city would be able to understand.

". . . dive, daughter, dive, and don't come up for air. Swim deep, little sister, swim deep . . ."

"What on earth are they talking about?" Arnie asked, looking up, surprised.

"That!" Nils said, looking out the port and turning his head swiftly to follow the silver swept-wing forms that flashed by below. "Russian MIG. We're just out of the clouds and I don't think they saw us. Can we drop any faster?"

"Hold on."

A twist of Arnie's fingers pushed their stomachs up into their throats.

"Let me know when we are about two hundred meters above the water," he said calmly. "So I can slow the drop before we hit."

Nils clutched the arms of his chair to keep from floating up despite his belt. The leaden surface of the Baltic flashed toward them, closer and closer, the waves with white caps were visible, and the *Vitus Bering* off to one side.

"Closer . . . closer . . . NOW!"

They were slammed down, loose equipment rolled, sliding across the suddenly canted deck. Then an even more powerful force crashed into the sub, jarring the entire hull, as they plunged beneath the surface.

"Will you please take over, Commander Wilhelmsen," Arnie said, and for the first time his voice was a bit uneven. "I am shutting down the Daleth unit."

The pumps throbbed to life and Henning almost caressed his control panel. It was hard to fly as a passenger in one's own submarine. He whistled between his teeth as he made a slow turn and angled up to periscope depth.

"Take a look through the periscope, will you, Hansen? It's easy enough to use, just like they do in the movies."

"Up periscope!" Nils chanted, slapping the handles down

and twisting his cap backward. He ground his face into the rubber cushion. "I can't see blast-all."

"Turn the knob to focus the lenses."

"Yes, that's better. The ship's off to port about thirty degrees." He swept the periscope in a circle. "No other ships in sight. This thing doesn't have a big enough field, so I can't tell about the sky."

"We'll have to take a chance. I'll bring her up a bit so the aerial is clear."

The radio hissed with background noise, then a voice broke in, died away and returned an instant later.

"Hello, Blaeksprutten, *can you hear me? Over. Hello . . ."*

"Blaeksprutten here. What's happening? Over."

"It is believed that you appeared on the Russian early warning radar screens. MIGs have been all over the area ever since you went up. None in sight now. We think that they did not see you come in. Please close on us and report on test. Over."

Arnie took up the microphone.

"Equipment functioned perfectly. No problems. Estimated height of a hundred fifty kilometers reached on battery power. Over."

He flicked the switch and the sound of distant cheering poured from the loudspeaker.

9

The table was littered with magazines and booklets that did not interest Horst Schmidt. ***Novy Mir, Russia Today, Pravda, Twelve Years of U.S. Imperialist Intervention and Aggression in Laos.*** He leaned back in the chair, resting his elbow on the journals, and drew deeply on his cigarette. A pigeon flapped and landed on the windowsill outside, turning a pink eye to look at him through the water-beaded pane. He tapped the cigarette on the edge of the ashtray and, at the sudden motion inside the room, the pigeon flew away. Schmidt turned as the door opened and Lidia Efimovna Shirochenka came into the room. She was a slim, blond-haired girl, who might have appeared Scandinavian had it not been for her high Slavic cheekbones. Her green tweed suit was well cut and fashionable, undoubtedly purchased in Denmark. Schmidt saw that she was reading his report, frowning over it.

"There is precious little here of any value," she said curtly, "considering the amount of money we pay you." She sat down behind the desk that bore a small plaque reading *Troisième Secrétaire de la Légation*. She spoke in German, utilizing this opportunity, as a good party member, to a dual advantage; gaining linguistic practice with a native speaker.

"There is a good deal of information there. Intelligence, even negative information, is still intelligence. We now know that the Americans are as much in the dark as we are about the affair at Langeliniekaj. We know that their fair-weather allies the Danes are not acquainting their NATO comrades with all of their internal secrets. We know that all of the armed forces seemed to be involved. And if you will carefully note the last paragraph, *tovarich* Shirochenka, you will see that I have tentatively identified one of the civilians who was aboard the *Isbjorn* during the same day when there was all that excitement. He is Professor Rasmussen, a Nobel prize winner in physics, which I find most interesting. What is the connection between this affair and a physicist?"

Lidia Shirochenka seemed unimpressed by this disclosure. She took a photograph from a drawer and passed it over to Schmidt. "Is that the man you are talking about?"

He had too many years of experience at guarding his expression to reveal any reaction—but he was very surprised. It was a very grainy picture, obviously taken with a telescopic lens under poor light conditions, yet good enough to be instantly recognizable. Ove Rasmussen, carrying a small case, was walking down a ramp from a ship.

"Yes, that's the same man. Where did you get this?"

"That is none of your business. You must realize that you are not the only man in the employ of this department. Your physicist now appears to be connected in some manner with rockets or missiles. Find out all you can about him. Who he sees, what he is doing. And do not tell the Americans about this little bit of information. That would be most unwise."

"You insult me! You know where my loyalty lies."

"Yes. With yourself. It is impossible to insult a double agent. I am just attempting to make it clear that it would be a drastic mistake for you to betray us in the same manner that you have betrayed your CIA employers. There is no loyalty for you, just money."

"On the contrary, I am most loyal." He snubbed out his cigarette, then took out his package and offered one to Lidia Shirochenka. She raised her eyes slightly at the label. American cigarettes were very expensive in Copenhagen. "Have one. I get them at PX discount, about a fifth of the usual price." He waited until he had lighted her cigarette before he continued.

"I am most loyal to your organization because it is the wisest arrangement for me. Speaking as a professional now, I can assure you that it is very difficult to get reliable intelligence information about the U.S.S.R. You have rigorous security procedures. Therefore I am happy for the items—I presume they are false—that you supply me for the Americans. They will never discover this because the CIA is hideously inefficient and has a one hundred percent record of never having ever been correct with intelligence information supplied to their own government. But they pay very well indeed for what they receive from me, and there are many fringe benefits." He held up his cigarette and smiled. "Not the least of which is the money you pay me for revealing their little secrets. I find it a profitable arrangement. Besides, I like your organization. Ever since Beria . . ."

"Things have changed a great deal since Beria," she said sharply. "A former SS man like yourself, an Oberst at Auschwitz has little claim to moral arguments." When he did not answer she turned to look out of the window, at the long white building barely visible through the light rainfall. She pointed.

"There they are, Schmidt, just across the graveyard from us. There is something very symbolic in that, have you never thought?"

"Never," he said emotionlessly. "You have far more insight into these matters than I have, *Tovarich* Shirochenka."

"Don't ever forget that. You are an employee whom we watch very closely. Try to get closer to this Professor Rasmussen . . ."

She broke off as the door opened. A young man in his shirtsleeves hurried in and handed her a piece of paper that had been torn from the teleprinter. She scanned it quickly and her eyes widened.

"Boshemoi!" she whispered, shocked. "It can't be true . . ."

The young man wordlessly nodded his head, the same look of numb disbelief on his face.

* * *

"How many hours now?" Arnie asked.

Ove looked at the chart hanging on the laboratory table. "Over two hundred fifty—and that is continuous operation. We seem to have most of the bugs worked out."

"I hope to say you do." Arnie admired the shining, cylindrical apparatus that almost filled the large workstand. It was festooned with wires and electronic plumbing, and flanked by a large control board. There was no sound of operation other than a low and distant humming. "This is quite a breakthrough," he added.

"The British did most of the groundwork back in the late sixties. I was interested because it related to some of my own work. I had been able to build up plasmas of two thousand degrees, but only for limited amounts of time, a few thousand microseconds. Then these people at Newcastle on Tyne began using a helium-caesium plasma at fourteen hundred sixty degrees centrigrade with an internal electric field. They were increasing the plasma conductivity up to a hundred times. I utilized their technique to build Little Hans here. I haven't been able to scale up the effect yet, not practically, but I think I see a way out. In any case Little Hans works fine and produces a few thousand volts steadily, so I cannot complain."

"You have done wonders." Arnie nodded thanks as one of the laboratory assistants handed him a cup of coffee. He stirred it slowly, thinking. "Scaled up this could be the power source we need for a true space vessel. A pressurized atomic generator, of the type now used in submarines and surface craft, would fit our needs. No fuel needed, no oxidant. But with one inherent drawback."

"Cooling," Ove said, and blew on his hot coffee.

"Exactly. You can cool with sea water in a ship, but that sort of thing is hard to come by in space. I suppose an external radiating unit could be constructed . . ."

"It would be far bigger than the ship itself!"

"Yes, I imagine it would. Which brings us back to your fusion generator. Plenty of power, not too much waste heat to bleed off. Will you let me help you with this?"

"Delighted. Between us I know . . ." He broke off, distracted by a sudden buzz of conversation from the far end of the laboratory. "Is there anything wrong down there?"

"I'm very sorry, Professor, it is just the news." She held up an early edition of BT.

"What's happened?"

"It's the Russians, that Moon-orbiting flight of theirs. It has turned out to be more than that, more than just a flight around the moon. It is a landing capsule, and they have set it down right in the middle of the Sea of Tranquility."

"The Americans won't be overjoyed about this," Ove said. "Up until now they have considered the Moon a bit of American landscape."

"That's the trouble." She held the newspaper out to them, her eyes wide. "They have landed, but something is wrong with their lunar module. They can't take off again."

There was little more to the newspaper report, other than the photograph of the three smiling cosmonauts that had been taken just before take-off. Nartov, Shavkun, and Zlotnikova. A colonel, a major, and a captain, in a neatly organized chain of command. Everything had been very well organized. Television coverage, reporters, take-off, first stage, second stage, radioed reports and thanks to Comrade Lenin for making the voyage possible, the approach, and the landing. They were down on the Moon's surface and they were alive. But something had gone wrong. What had happened was not clear from the reports, but the result was obvious enough. The men were down. Trapped. There for good. They would live just as long as their oxygen lasted.

"What an awful way to die, so far from home," the laboratory assistant said, speaking for all of them.

Arnie thought, thought slowly and considered what had happened. His eyes went to the fusion generator, and when he looked back he found that Ove had been looking at it too, as though they both shared the same idea.

"Come on," Ove said, looking at his watch. "Let's go home. There's nothing more to be done here today, and if we leave now we can beat most of the traffic."

Neither of them talked as Ove pulled the car through the stream of bicycles and turned north on Lyngbyvej. They had the radio on and listened to the news most of the way to Charlottenlund.

"You two are home early," Ulla said when they came in. She was Ove's wife, a still attractive redhead, although she was in her mid-forties. While Arnie was staying with them she had more than a slight tendency to mother him, thinking he was far too thin. She took instant advantage of this unexpected opportunity. "I'm just making tea and I'll bring you in some. And some sandwiches to hold you until dinner." She ignored all protests and hurried out.

They went into the living room and switched on the television. The Danish channel had not come on the air yet, but Sweden was broadcasting a special program about the cosmonauts and they listened closely to this. Details were being released, almost grudgingly, by Moscow, and the entire tragedy could now be pieced together.

The landing had been a good one right up to the very end.

Setdown had been accomplished in the exact area that had been selected and, until the moment of touchdown, it had looked perfect. But as the engines cut off one of the tripod landing legs had given way. Details were not given, whether the leg itself had broken or gone into a hole, but the results were clear enough. The lunar module had fallen over on its side. One of the engines had been torn free: an undisclosed quantity of fuel had been lost. The module would not be able to take off. The cosmonauts were down to stay.

"I wonder if the Soviets have a backup rocket that could get there?" Arnie asked.

"I doubt it. They would have mentioned it if there were any chance. You heard those deep Slavic tones of tragedy in the interview. If there were any hope at all it would have been mentioned. They are already written off, and busts are being made of them for the Hall of Fame."

"What about the Americans?"

"If they could do anything they would jump at the chance, but they have said nothing. Even if they had a ship ready to go, which they probably don't, they don't have a window. This is the completely wrong time of the month for them to attempt a lunar trip. By the time there is a window that trio of cosmonauts will be dead."

"Then . . . nothing can be done?"

"Here's your tea," Ulla said, bringing in the heavily loaded tray.

"You know better than that," Ove told him. "You have been thinking the same thing I have. Why don't we take the fusion generator, put it in *Blaeksprutten*—and go up there to the Moon and rescue them."

"It sounds an absolutely insane idea when you come right out and say it."

"It's an insane world we live in. Shall we give it a try—see if we can talk the Minister into it?"

"Why not?" Arnie raised his cup. "To the Moon, then."

"To the Moon!"

Ulla, eyes wide, looked back and forth from one to the other as though she thought they were both mad.

10

THE MOON

"Signing off until sixteen hundred hours for next contact," Colonel Nartov said, and threw the switch on the radio. He wore sunglasses and ragged-bottom shorts, hacked from his nylon shipsuit, and nothing else. His dark whiskers were now long enough to feel soft when he rubbed at them, having finally grown out of the scratchy stage. They itched too, not for the first time he wished that there was enough water to have a good scrub. He felt hot and sticky all over, and the tiny cabin reeked like a bear pit.

Shavkun was asleep, breathing hoarsely through his gaping mouth. Captain Zlotnikova was fiddling with the knobs on the receiver—they had more than enough power from their solar panels—looking for the special program that was beamed to them night and day. There was static, a blare of music, then the gentle melody of a balalaika playing an old folk melody. Zlotnikova leaned back, arms behind his head, and hummed a quiet accompaniment. Nartov looked up at the blue and white mottled globe in the black sky and felt a strong desire for a cigarette. Shavkun groaned in his sleep and made smacking noises with his mouth.

"Chess?" Nartov asked, and Zlotnikova laid down the well-worn thin-paper copy of *The Collected Works of V.I. Lenin* that he had been leafing through. It was the only book aboard—they had planned to read from it when they planted the Soviet flag in Lunar soil—and, while inspiring in other circumstances, bore little relationship to their present condition. Chess was better. The little pocket set was the most important piece of equipment aboard *Vostoj IV*.

"I'm four games ahead of you," Nartov said, passing over the board. "You're white."

Zlotnikova nodded and played a safe and sane pawn to king

four. The colonel was a strong player and he was taking no chances. The sun, pouring down on the Sea of Tranquility outside, hung apparently motionless in the black sky, although it crept closer to the horizon all the time. Even with sunglasses he squinted against the glare, automatically looking for some movement, some change in that ocean of rock and sand, mother-of-pearl, grayish green, lifeless.

"Your move." He looked back at the board, moved his knight.

"A vacuum, airless . . . whoever thought it would be this hot?" Zlotnikova said.

"Whoever thought we would be here this long, as I have told you before. As highly polished as this ship is, some radiation still gets through. It hasn't a hundred percent albedo. So we warm up. We were suppospd to be here less than a day, it wasn't considered important."

"It is after eleven days. Guard your queen."

The colonel wiped the sweat from his forehead with the back of his arm, looked out at the changeless moonscape, looked back to the board. Shavkun grunted and opened his eyes.

"Too damn hot to sleep," he mumbled.

"That hasn't seemed to bother you the last couple of hours," Zlotnikova said, then castled queenside to get away from the swiftly mounting kingside attack.

"Watch your tongue, Captain," Shavkun said, irritable after the heat-sodden sleep.

"I'm a Hero of the Soviet People," Zlotnikova answered, unimpressed by the reprimand. Rank meant very little now.

Shavkun looked distastefully at the other two, heads bent over the board. He was a really second-rate player himself. The other two beat him so easily that it had been decided to leave him out of the contest. This gave him too much time to think in.

"How long before the oxygen runs out?"

Nartov shrugged, bearlike and fatalistic, without bothering to look up from the board. "Two days, maybe a third. We'll know better when we have to crack the last cylinder."

"And then what?"

"And then we will decide about it," he said with quick irritation. Playing the game had put the unavoidable from his mind for a few minutes; he did not enjoy being dragged back to it. "We have already talked about it. Dying by asphyxiation can be painful. There are a lot simpler ways. We'll discuss it then."

Shavkun slid from the bunk and leaned against the viewport, which was canted at a slight angle. They had managed to level off the vessel by digging at the other two legs, but nothing could replace the lost fuel. And there was the Earth, looking so close. He pulled the camera from its clip and squinted through the pentaprism, using their strongest telescopic lens.

"That storm is over. The entire Baltic is clear. I do believe I can even see Leningrad. It's clear, really clear there with the sun shining. . . ."

"Shut up," Colonel Nartov said sharply, and he did.

11

The gray waters of the Baltic hissed along the side of the *MS Vitus Bering*, breaking into mats of foam that were swept quickly astern. A seagull flapped slowly alongside, an optimistic eye open for any garbage that might be thrown overboard. Arnie stood at the rail, welcoming the sharp morning air after the night in the musty cabin. The sky, still banded with red in the east where the sun was pushing its edge over the horizon, was almost cloudless, its pale blue bowl resting on the heaving plain of the sea. The door creaked open and Nils came on deck, yawning and stretching. He cocked a professional eye out from under the brim of his uniform cap—his Air Force one, not SAS this time—and looked around.

"Looks like good flying weather, Professor Klein."

"Arnie, if you please, Captain Hansen. As shipmates on this important flight I feel there should be less formality."

"Nils. You're right, of course. And, by God, it *is* important, I'm just beginning to realize that. All the planning is one thing, but the thought that we are leaving for the Moon after breakfast and will be there before lunch . . . It's a little hard to accept." The mention of food reminded him of the vacant space in his great frame. "Come on, let's get some of that breakfast before it's all gone."

There was more than enough left. Hot cereal and cold cereal; Nils had a little of each, sprinkling the uncooked oatmeal over his cornflakes and drowning them both in milk in the Scandinavian manner. This was followed by boiled eggs, four kinds of bread, a platter of cheese, ham, and salami. For those with even better appetites there were three kinds of herring, Arnie, more used to the light Israeli breakfast, settled for some dark bread and butter and a cup of coffee. He looked with fascinated interest as the big pilot had one serving of everything to try it out, then went around again for seconds. Ove came in, poured some coffee, and joined them at the table.

"The three of us are the crew," he said. "It's all set. I was up half the night with Admiral Sander-Lange and he finally saw the point."

"What is the point?" Nils asked, talking around a large mouthful of herring and buttered *rugbrod*. "I'm a pilot, so you must have me, but is there any reason to have two high-powered physicists aboard?"

"No real reason," Ove answered, ready with the answer after a night of debating the point. "But there are two completely separate devices aboard—the Daleth drive and the fusion generator—and each requires constant skilled attention. It just so happens that we are the only two people for the job, sort of high-paid mechanics, and that is what is important. The physicist part is secondary at this point. If *Blaeksprutten* is to fly, we are the only ones who can fly her. We've come so far now that we can't turn back. Our risk is really negligible—compared to the certain death facing those cosmonauts on the Moon. And it's also a matter of honor now. We know we can do it. We have to try."

"Danish honor," Nils said gravely, then broke into a wide grin. "This is really going to rock the Russians back on their heels! How many people in their country? Two hundred twenty-six or two hundred twenty-seven million, too many to count. And how many in all of Denmark?"

"Under five million."

"Correct—a lot less than in Moscow alone. So they have all their parades and rockets and boosters and speeches and politicians, and their thing falls over and all the juice runs out. So we come along and pick up the pieces!"

The ship's officers at the next table had been silent, listening as Nils's voice grew louder with enthusiasm. Now they burst out in applause, laughing aloud. This flight appealed to the Danish sense of humor. Small they were, but immensely proud, with a long and fascinating history going back a thousand years. And, like all the Baltic countries, they were always aware of the Soviet Union just across that small, shallow sea. This rescue attempt would be remembered for a long time to come. Ove looked at his watch and stood up.

"It is less than two hours to our first lift-off computation. Let us see if we can make it."

They finished quickly and hurried on deck. The submarine was already out of the hold and in the water, with technicians aboard making the last-minute arrangements.

"With all these changes the tub really needs a new name," Nils said. "Maybe *Den Flyvende Blaeksprutte*—the Flying Squid. It has a nice ring to it."

Henning Wilhelmsen climbed back over the rail and joined them, his face set in lines of unalloyed glumness. Since he knew her best, he had supervised all of the equipment changes and installations.

"I don't know what she is now—a spaceship I guess. But she's no longer a sub. No power plant, no drive units. I had to pull out the engine to make room for that big tin pressure hull!" This last crime was the end of the world to any submariner. Nils clapped him on the back.

"Cheer up—you've done your part. You have changed her from a humble larva into a butterfly of the skies."

"Very poetical." Henning refused to be cheered up. "She's more of a luna moth than a butterfly now. Take good care of her."

"You can be sure of that," Nils said, sincerely. "It's my own skin that I'm worried about, and *Den Flyvende Blaeksprutte* is the only transportation around. All changes finished?"

"All done. You have an air-pressure altimeter now, as well as a radio altimeter. Extra oxygen tanks, air-scrubbing equipment, a bigger external aerial, everything they asked for and more. We even put lunch aboard for you, and the admiral donated a bottle of *snaps*. Ready to go." He reached out and shook the pilot's hand. "Good luck."

"See you later tonight."

There was much handshaking then, last-minute instructions, and a rousing cheer as they went aboard and closed the hatch. A Danish flag had been painted on the conning tower and it gleamed brightly in the early morning sun.

"Dogged tight," Nils said, giving an extra twist to the wheel that sealed the hatch above, set into the conning tower's deck.

"What about the hatch on top of the tower?" Ove asked.

"Closed but not sealed, as you said. The air will bleed out of the conning tower long before we get there."

"Fine. That's about as close to an airlock as we can rig on a short notice. Now, are we all certain that we know what to do and how to do it?"

"I know," Nils grumbled, "but I miss the checklists."

"The Wright brothers didn't have checklists. We'll save that for those who follow after. Arnie, can we run through the drill once more?"

"Yes, of course. We have a computation coming up in about twenty minutes, and I see no reason why we should not make it." He went forward to look out of a port. "The ship is moving away to give us plenty of room." He pointed down at the controls in front of Nils, most of them newly mounted on top of the panel.

"Nils, you are the pilot. I have rigged controls here for you that will enable you to change course. We have gone over them so you know how they operate. We will have to work together on take-offs and landings, because those will have to be done from the Daleth unit, which I will man. Ove is our engine room and will see to it that we have a continuous supply of current. The batteries are still here, and charged, but they will be saved for emergencies. Which I sincerely hope we will not have. I will make the vertical take-off and get us clear of the atmosphere. Nils will put us on our course and keep us on it. I will control acceleration. If the university computer that ties in with the radar operates all right, they should tell us when to reverse thrust. If they do not tell us, we shall have to reverse by chronometer and do the best we can by ourselves."

"Now that is the part I *don't* understand," Nils said, pushing his cap back on his head and pointing to the periscope. "This is a plain old underwater periscope—now modified so that it looks straight up rather than ahead. It had a cross hair in it. I'm supposed to get a star in the cross hair and keep it there, and you want me to believe that this is all we have to navigate by? Shouldn't there be a navigator?"

"An astrogator, if you want to be precise."

"An astrogator then. Someone who can plot a course for us?"

"Someone whom you can have a little more faith in than a periscope you mean?" Ove asked, laughing, and opened the door to the engine compartment.

"Exactly. I'm thinking about all those course corrections, computations, and such that the Americans and Soviets have done before to get to the Moon. Can we really do it with this?"

"We have the same computations behind us, realize that. But we have a much simpler means of applying them because of the shorter duration of our flight. When time is allowed for our initial slower speed through the atmosphere, our flying time is almost exactly four hours. Knowing this, certain prominent stars were picked as targets and the computations were made. Those are our computation times. If we leave at the correct moment and keep the target star in the sight all of the time, we will be aiming at the spot in the Moon's orbit where it will be at the end of the four hours. We both move to our appointed meeting place. and the descent can be made. After we locate the Soviet capsule, that is."

"And that is going to be easy?" Nils asked, looking dubious.

"I don't see why not," Ove answered, poking his head out of the engine cubby, wiping his hands on a rag. "The generator is operating and the output is right on the button." He pointed to the large photograph of the Moon pasted to the front bulkhead. "Goodness, we know what the Moon looks like, we've all looked through telescopes and can find the Sea of Tranquility. We go there, to the right spot, and if we don't see the Soviets we use the direction finder to track them down."

"And at what spot do we look in the Sea of Tranquility? Do we follow this?" Nils pointed to the blurry photograph of the Moon that had been cut from the newspaper *Pravda*. There was a red star printed in the north of the *mare* where the cosmonauts had landed. "*Pravda* says this is where they are. Do we navigate from a *newspaper* photo?"

"We do unless you can think of something better," Arnie said mildly. "And do not forget our direction finder is a standard small boat model bought from A.P. Moller Ship Supplies in Copenhagen. Does that bother you too?"

After one last scowl Nils burst out laughing. "The whole thing is so outrageous that it just has to succeed." He fastened his lap belt. "*Blaeksprutten* to the rescue!"

"It is all much more secure than it might look," Ove explained. "You must remember that we had this operational submarine to begin with. It is a sealed, tested, proven, self-sufficient spaceship built for a different kind of space. But it works just as well in a vacuum as under water. And the Daleth drive is operational and reliable—and will get us to the Moon in a few hours. The combination of radar and computer on Earth will track us and compute the correct course for us to follow. Everthing possible has been done to make this trip a safe one. There will be later voyages and the instrumentation will be refined, but we have all we need now to get us safely to the Moon and back. So don't worry."

"Who is worrying?" Nils said. "I always sweat and get pale at this time of day. Is it time to leave yet?"

"A few more minutes to go," Arnie said, looking at the electronic chronometer before him. "I am going to take off and get a bit of altitude."

His fingers moved across the controls and the deck pressed up against them. The waves dropped away. Tiny figures were visible aboard the *Vitus Bering*, waving enthusiastically, then they shrank and vanished from sight as *Blaekspruttеn* hurled itself, faster and faster, into the sky.

The strangest thing about the voyage was its utter uneventfulness. Once clear of the atmosphere they accelerated at a constant one G. And one gravity of acceleration cannot be sensed as being different in any way from the gravity experienced on the surface of the Earth. Behind them, like a toy, or the projection on a large-size screen, the globe of the Earth shrank away. There was no thunder of rockets or roar of engines, no bouncing or air pockets. Since the ship was completely sealed, there was not even the small drop in atmospheric pressure that is felt in a commercial airliner. The equipment worked perfectly and, once clear of the Earth's atmospheric envelope, their speed increased.

"On course—or at least we are aimed at the target star," Nils said. "I think we can check with Copenhagen now and see if they are tracking us. It would be nice to know if we are going in the right direction." He switched the transceiver to the preset frequency and called in the agreed rode.

"*Kylling* calling *Halvabe*. Can you read me? Over." He threw the switch. "I wonder what drunk thought up these code names," he mumbled to himself. The sub was the "chick" and the other station the "lemur"—but these names were also slang terms for a quarter-litre and a half-litre bottle of akvavit.

"We read you loud and clear, Kylling. *You are on course, though your acceleration is slightly more than optimum. Suggest a five percent reduction."*

"Roger. Will conform. Are you tracking us?"

"Positive."

"Will you send turnover signal?"

"Positive."

"Over and out." He killed the power. "Did you hear that? Things couldn't be better."

"I have cut the acceleration by the five percent," Arnie said. "Yes, things could not be better."

"Would anyone like a Carlsberg?" Ove asked. "Someone has stuffed a whole case back here." He passed a can to Nils, but Arnie declined.

"Finish them quickly," he said. "We are not far from turnover, and I cannot guarantee that things will not get shaken up a bit. I could reduce the thrust to zero before I turned the ship, but that would put us in free fall for awhile and I would like to avoid that if I could. Aside from our personal feelings, the equipment just isn't designed for it. Instead, I shall attempt to rotate the ship one hundred eighty degrees while maintaining full thrust, at which point we will begin to decelerate."

"Sounds fine to me," Nils said, squinting through the periscope and making a precise adjustment. "But what about our course? Is that what we use this gas pipe in the deck for? The one that Henning was moaning about because it needed a hole in his pressure hull?"

"That is correct. There is a wide-angle lens system here, with an optical gunsight fitted into it."

"The kind used on fighter planes to fire the guns?"

"Precisely. You will keep the star centered as before. I envisage no problems."

"No, no problems at all." Nils looked around at the jury-rigged and hurriedly converted sub and shook his head in wonder. "Will one of you take the con for me for a minute? I have to go to the head. The beer, you know."

Turnover went smoothly, and they would not have known they were rotating if they hadn't watched the sunlight move across the deck and up the bulkhead. A few loose objects rattled, and a pencil rolled across the desk and fell.

Time moved swiftly. The sun glared and there was some discussion of solar storms and Van Allen radiation. These were no serious menace since the pressure hull of the submarine was a solid metal barrier, incredibly thicker than that of any rocket ever launched.

"Have you thought about talking to the cosmonauts?" Ove asked. He stood in the doorway of the engine compartment where he could watch the fusion generator and talk with the others at the same time.

"They are all pilots," Nils said. "So they should speak English." Ove disagreed.

"Only if they have flown out of the country. Inside the Soviet Union Aeroflot uses Russian. Only on international flights is English required for radio control. I put in six months there, at Moscow University, so I can talk to them if I have to. I was hoping that one of you was more fluent."

"Hebrew, English, Yiddish, or German," Arnie said. "That's all."

"Just English, Swedish, and French," Nils told them. "It looks like it is up to you, Ove."

Like most Europeans with college education they took it for granted that one spoke at least one language other than his own. Like Scandinavians, two or three other languages were more likely. They assumed that the cosmonauts would speak something they could understand.

The computer kept track of their progress and, when the four hours were nearing their end, they were informed that they could turn on their radio altimeter because they were nearing the point where it would be effective. Its maximum range was a hundred and fifty kilometers.

"Getting a fringe reading," Nils called, excited. "The Moon is down there all right." Since midpoint they had not seen the satellite which was beneath their keel.

"Let me know when we are about a hundred kilometers above the surface," Arnie said. "I'll roll the ship then so we can see through the side ports."

There was a growing tension now as the spacegoing submarine hurtled down toward the Moon, still out of sight below them.

"The altimeter is unwinding pretty fast," Nils said, his controlled pilot's voice showing none of the tension he felt.

"I'll raise the deceleration up to two G's," Arnie said. "Stand by."

It was a strange sensation, as though they were suddenly growing heavier, with their arms pulled down and their chins sinking to their chests: their chairs creaked and their breathing labored. Nils moved his hand to the controls, and it felt as though weights hung from his arm. He weighed over four hundred pounds now. "Rate of drop slowing," he said. "Coming up on a hundred kilometers. Rate of drop slowing to near zero."

"I'm going to hover at this altitude while we look for the target area," Arnie said. Thankfully. He was too obviously aware of the thudding of his heart as it labored to pump blood in the doubled gravity. As he adjusted the controls weight fell away, to one gravity, and past that, until it felt as though they would float free. Hovering now, they were in the grip of the Moon's gravitic field, a mere one-sixth of that of the Earth. "Rotating," he said.

Loose objects rolled across the deck and clattered against the wall as they tilted over; they clung to the arms of their chairs. White light flooded in through the port.

"Ih, du Almaegtige!" Nils whispered. There it was. Filling the sky. Less than seventy miles below them. Cratered, streaked, pitted, dead and airless, another world. The Moon.

"Then we've done it," Ove said. "Done it!" he shouted with rising excitement. "By God we've crossed space in this tub and we've reached the Moon." He unhooked his belt and stood, staggering as he tried to walk in the lessened gravity. Sliding, half falling, he slammed into the bulkhead, unheeding, as he braced himself to look out of the port.

"Just look at that, will you! Copernicus, the Sea of Storms, now where would the Sea of Tranquility be? To the east, in that direction." He shaded his eyes against the reflected glare. "We can't see it yet, but it has to be that way. Over the curve of the horizon."

Silent as a falling leaf *Blaeksprutten* tilted back to the horizontal, then rotated about an invisible axis. They had to lean back to balance themselves as the bow swung down and the Moon reappeared, this time directly ahead.

"Is that enough of an angle for you to see to navigate by?" Arnie asked.

"Fine. There's worse visibility from an airliner."

"Then I shall hold this attitude and this height and switch forward and lateral control to your position."

"On the way." Nils hummed happily to himself as he pressed gently on his control wheel."

* * *

The three cosmonauts stood to attention as best they could in the cramped module with limited floor space: Zlotnikova had his nose pressed practically against the colonel's hairy shoulder. The last notes of "The Internationale" died away and the radio speaker hissed gently with static.

"At ease," Nartov ordered, and the other two dropped into their bunks while he picked up the microphone and switched it on. "In the name of my fellow cosmonauts, I thank you. They stand behind me, and agree with me, when in this moment of victory, I say that you, fellow citizens of the Union of Soviet Socialist Republics, should not grieve. This is a victory for us all; for the Party Chairman, Members of the Presidium, workers in the factories where parts of the rocket and capsule were manufactured, to be assembled by . . ."

Lieutenant Zlotnikova's attention wandered: he had never been one for either making speeches or listening to them. Stolidly, he had listened to thousands upon thousands of hours of speeches during his twenty-eight years on Earth. And on the Moon. They were an accepted evil, like snow in the winter and drought in the summer. They were there, whether one liked it or not, and nothing could be done about them. Best to ignore them and suffer them, which was where a fatalistic, Slavic state of mind helped. He was a fighter pilot, one of the best, and a cosmonaut, one of the few. Attaining these goals was worth any sacrifice. Listening to speeches was only a minor bother. Even death was not too high a price to pay. He had no regrets; the game was worth the candle. But he just wished it could be done with a few less speeches. The colonel's voice droned on and he glanced out of the viewport, then turned quickly away since at least an appearance of courtesy was called for. But the colonel had his back turned, with his right fist clenched in a salute and marking time to the strong rhythm of his words. It must be a good speech. At least the colonel was enjoying it. Zlotnikova turned back to the port—then tensed abruptly at the slowly moving speck of light high above. A meteor? Moving so slowly?

". . . and how many died in battle to preserve the freedom of our great land? The Red Army never hesitated to embrace death for the greater good, peace, freedom, liberty, and victory. Should Soviet cosmonauts shirk responsibilities, or ignore the realities of"—angrily he brushed away the bothersome hand that was tapping him on the shoulder. ". . . the realities of space flight, of the complexity . . ."

"Colonel!"

"—the complexity of the program, the great machines, the responsibilities . . ." *Bothering him in the middle of this speech—was the bastard mad?* ". . . to all the Soviet workers who made possible . . ."

Colonel Nartov wheeled about to glare and silence the lieutenant. But his gaze followed Zlotnikova's pointing finger to the port, through the thick glass, across the cratered, airless moonscape to the small submarine which was slowly settling down out of the star-flecked sky.

The colonel coughed, gasped, cleared his throat, and looked at the microphone in his hand with something resembling horror. "I will complete this call later," he said abruptly, and switched off. "What the hell is that?" he roared.

For obvious reasons, neither of the other men answered. They were shocked, silent, and the only sound was the whispering of their last bit of depleted atmosphere coming through the grill, the mutter from the radio of distant music as someone back on Earth started the band playing again to cover the untimely silence from the Moon.

Slowly the submarine settled, no more than fifty meters from their capsule, hovering daintily the last few centimeters above the gravel before easing itself down. There were some strands of very dehydrated seaweed plastered to its keel, thin streaks of rust at the stern.

"Danish?" Shavkun gasped, pointing to the flag painted on the small conning tower. "That is Danish, isn't it?" Zlotnikova nodded, silently, then realized that his jaw was gaping open and closed it with a sharp click. The radio rustled and squealed, and a voice came in over the music in very loud, very bad, Russian.

"*Hello* Vostok IV, *can you read me*? *This is* Blaeksprutten, *and I have landed near you. Can you read me*? *Over.*"

Colonel Nartov looked at the microphone in his hand and started to turn it on. He stopped and shook his head, trying to rally his thoughts, then reached for the radio controls. Only after he had cut the output power to a trickle did he switch on the transmitter. For some automatic defensive reason, he did not wish Moscow to hear this conversation.

"This is *Vostok IV*. Colonel Nartov. Who is that speaking? Who are you? What are you doing here—" The colonel cut himself off abruptly, feeling that he was about to start babbling.

Aboard *Blaeksprutten*, Ove listened and nodded. "Contact established," he told the others. "Better put that curtain up now while I get them over here." He switched the radio on. *"Govoreetye vy po Angleeskee?"* he asked.

"Yes, I speak English."

"Very good, Colonel," Ove said, changing with some relief to that language. "I am pleased to tell you that we are here to bring you back to Earth. In your broadcast a few minutes ago you said that all three of you are all right. Is that true?"

"Of course, but . . ."

"That's fine. If you would get into your spacesuits . . ."

"Yes, but you must tell me . . ."

"First things first, if you please, Colonel. Do you think you could put on your suit and step over here for a minute? I would come myself, but unhappily we don't have any space gear. If you don't mind?"

"I am on my way." There was a certain positiveness in the way the message ended.

"The colonel didn't sound so happy for a man whose life had just been saved," Nils said, threading the line through the grommets in the large tarpaulin that was spread out on the dock. It was gray and weatherstained, with a certain memory of fish lingering about it, perhaps from being stored near the marine life specimens in the hold of the *Vitus Bering*.

"He's happy enough, I imagine," Ove said, going to help the others with the clumsy canvas. "But I guess it will take a little getting used to. He was in the middle of a very dramatic sort of deathbed speech when we interrupted."

They threaded the lines through ringbolts in the ceiling and hauled it up. It made a wrinkled barrier the width of the small cabin, cutting off sight of the Daleth unit and the fusion generator.

"Better not tie down this corner," Ove said. "I have to get past it to reach the engine compartment."

"It doesn't seem a very effective barrier," Nils said.

"It will do," Arnie told him. "These men are officers and presumably gentlemen—and we are saving their lives. I do not think they will cause any trouble."

"No, I guess not. . . ." Nils looked out of the port. "Say, their lock is opening—and here comes someone. Probably the colonel."

Colonel Nartov still had not adjusted to the changed circumstances. He had put on his spacesuit with automatic motions, ignoring the excited speculation of the other two cosmonauts, then stood calmly while they checked and sealed it. Now, jumping the last few feet to the surface of the Moon, he took a grip on himself. This was really happening. They were not going to die. He would see Moscow, his wife and family, again, and that was a pleasant thought. This strange craft had come to the Moon so it could undoubtedly return to Earth. Details would be explained later. Bringing his men back alive was his first concern. Head up, he strode toward the submarine, the dust and pebbles kicked up by his thick-soled boots falling back instantly to the airless surface.

A man was visible in the round port above, wearing a peaked cap of some kind, pointing downward with his finger and nodding his head. What on Earth—or the Moon—could it mean?

When the colonel came closer he saw that a thick-lidded box had been hurriedly welded to the hull. It was labeled **телефон** in black Cyrillic characters. He loosened the large thumb screw that held the cover into place, then swung it open and took out the telephone handset that was on a bracket inside. When he pressed it hard against his helmet the vibrations of his voice carried through well enough, and he could understand the man on the other end.

"Can you hear me, Colonel?"

"Yes." The cord was long enough so that when he stepped back he could see the man with another telephone through the port above.

"Good. I'm Captain Nils Hansen, Danish Air Force, Senior Danish Captain with SAS. I'll introduce the others when you come aboard. Can you reach the deck above you?"

The colonel squinted upward against the glare. "Not now. But we can attach a rope, working together, or something. The gravity is very light."

"It shouldn't be hard. Once on deck you will find that there is a hatch on top of the conning tower, unsealed. The conning tower is just big enough to hold three men, with crowding, and you will all have to come in at once since it is not a proper airlock. Get in, seal the top hatch just as tightly as you can, then knock three times on the deck. We'll let the air in then. Can you do this?"

"Of course."

"Can you bring whatever oxygen you have left? We don't want to run short on the return trip. We should have enough, but it doesn't hurt to have some extra."

"We will do that. We have a last cylinder that we have just tapped."

"One final thing before you go. We have some—secret equipment aboard, out of sight behind a screen. We would like to ask you to avoid going near it."

"You have my word," the colonel said, drawing himself up. "And my officers will give you their word as well." He looked at the big-jawed, smiling man through the thick port and, for the first time, the reality of this last-minute reprieve struck home to him. "I would like to thank you, for all of us, for what you are doing. You have saved our lives."

"We are glad to be here, and very happy that we could do it. Now . . ."

"We will be back. In very few minutes."

When he returned to the capsule, the colonel could see the two faces watching him through the port, close together, pressed to the glass like children at the window of a candy store. He almost smiled, but stopped himself in time.

"Get your suits on," he said when he had cycled through the lock. "We are going home. Those Danes are taking us." He switched on the radio and picked up the microphone in order to silence their stammered questions. The distant band, now playing "Meadowland," moaned and died as his call went out.

"Yes, Vostok IV, *we hear you. Is there any difficulty? Your last message was interrupted. Over."*

The colonel frowned, then switched on.

"This is Colonel Nartov. This is a final message. I am switching off and closing communication now."

"Colonel, please, we know how you feel. All Russia is with you in spirit. But the General wishes—"

"Tell the General that I will contact him later. Not by radio." He took a deep breath and kept his thumb on the switch. "I have his Kremlin telephone number. I will call him from Denmark." He switched off quickly and killed the power. Should he have said more? What *could* he have said that would have made sense? Other countries would be listening.

"Oh hell," he snapped at his two wide-eyed companions. "Major, get the log books, film, records, samples, put them into a box. Lieutenant, close the oxygen cylinder and unship it so we can take it with us. We'll go on suit oxygen now. Any questions?" There was only silence, so he snapped his face-plate closed.

"Here they come," Nils called out a few minutes later. "The last one just climbed down, and they have closed the airlock. They are bundled down with a lot of junk, records and such I imagine, one of them even has a camera. Say—he's taking pictures of us!"

"Let them," Ove said. "They can't learn a thing from the photographs. You know, we should have some specimens too. Before they climb aboard get the colonel on the phone again. Tell him we want some rocks and dirt, something to take home."

"Specimens brought back by the First Danish Lunar Expedition. Good idea, since we can't go outside ourselves. How is it going?"

"Fine," Ove said, opening a bottle of akvavit and placing it beside the little glasses on the map table. "We should have thought to bring some vodka, but I bet we'll hear no complaints about this *snaps*." He opened one of the *smorrebrod* containers that the cook had packed that morning, and slid out the open-faced sandwiches inside. "The herring is still fresh, they'll like that, and there's liver paste here as well."

"I'll eat it myself if they don't get here pretty soon," Nils said, eyeing the food hungrily. "Here they come."

He waved cheerfully through the port at the three laden figures trudging across the lunar plain.

12

COPENHAGEN

The Minister of Foreign Affairs shuffled through the notes he had made during the conference with the Prime Minister, finally finding the quote he wanted.

"Read back the last sentence, will you please?" he said.

"The Prime Minister does appreciate your exceedingly kind communication, and . . ." His secretary flipped the page in her steno book and waited, pencil poised.

"And has asked me to thank you for the good wishes you

expressed. He feels that it was very gracious of you to offer access to all of your advanced technologies in space engineering and rocketry, in addition to the use of your extended network of tracking stations around the globe. However, since we have little or nothing that we could contribute to a rocketry program, we feel that it would be unfair of us to enter into any agreements at this time. That's all. The usual salutations and close. Would you read the whole thing back to me?"

He swung his chair around and looked out of the window while she read. It was dark, the streets empty with the rush-hour crowds long gone. Seven o'clock. Too late for dinner. He would have to stop for something before he went home. He nodded his head as the pontifical weight of the words rolled out. All in order, just right. Thanks a lot but no thanks. The Soviets would happily turn over all their billions of rubles of useless rocket hardware in exchange for a peek at the Daleth drive. They weren't getting it. Neither were the Americans, though they seemed to have a stronger case; ties of brotherhood, NATO partners, and the sharing of defense secrets among partners. It had been something to watch the American ambassador getting redder and redder as the Prime Minister ticked off on his fingers ten American major defense projects that the Danes knew nothing at all about. The whole world wanted a cut from the cake.

"That's fine," he said when the girl stopped.

"Should I type it now, sir?"

"Not on your life. First thing in the morning, and have it on my desk when I get in. Now get home before your family forgets what you look like."

"Thank you, sir. Good night."

"Good night."

She click-clicked out, her high heels sounding clearly across the outer office in the silence of the empty ministry building. The door slammed. He yawned and stretched, then began to stuff papers into his briefcase. He sealed it and, before he put his coat on, phoned down for his car. The very last thing, he checked the file cabinets to see that they were all locked, and gave the lock on his safe an extra spin. That was enough. He set his big black hat squarely on his head, picked up his briefcase and left. It had been a long day and he was tired; he walked with a heavy, measured pace.

The slow footsteps passed by outside the door and Horst Schmidt shifted in the darkness. His knees were stiff and sore, while his legs burned like fire from standing still so long. He was getting a little old for this kind of thing. But it paid so well. In fact he looked forward to being paid exceedingly well for this night's work. He lifted his arm and examined the glowing face of his watch. 7:15. They should all be gone by now. The two sets of footsteps he had heard were the only ones in over a half an hour. Perhaps he should wait longer, but his legs wouldn't let him. Over three hours standing in this damn supply closet. He took up his thick briefcase and felt for the lock, turned it silently and opened the door a crack, blinking at the sudden light. The hall was empty when he looked out.

No security these Danes, no security at all. He closed the door behind him and walked, swiftly and soundlessly on his gum soles, to the office of the Minister of Foreign Affairs. The door was unlocked! They almost invited one in. A name—taken from the phone book—and an imaginary appointment had gotten him by the concierge at the front door. They had not even asked for a card, though he had one ready, but had settled simply for the false name he gave. Danes! The Minister's private office was unlocked as well—and the door did not even have a bolt on the inside. He opened his briefcase and, feeling in the darkness, took out a wooden wedge which he jammed into the crack between the door and the frame.

There were two thin, but completely opaque, plastic sheets in his case, and he draped these over the door and window, sealing them down with sticking tape. Only then did he turn on the powerful torch. The files first, there were sure to be a lot of interesting items in the files. The Daleth drive was of course the main interest, but there were plenty of other things he would like to know, information that could be fed to his employers, bit by bit, to assure a steady income. Spreading out his tools, he selected a chrome steel jimmy with a razor-sharp end. One twist of this opened the file cabinet as though it were a sardine can. With quick precision he flipped through the folders. A little pile of paper grew on the table next to him.

The safe would be a little more difficult—but not very. An antique. He studied it for a few moments, pulling the wrinkles out of his thin gloves as he considered the quickest way to open it.

Because of the soundproofing on it the drill was bulkier than most. But it was geared down and powerful. His bits were diamond tipped. He slapped a handful of clay onto the lock and pushed the bit into it: this would absorb most of the drilling sound. There was just the thinnest whine and vibration when he switched it on. It took only moments to hole through the steel plate.

What came next could be dangerous, but Schmidt was very experienced in taking care of his own skin. With Teutonic neatness he put all of his tools back into the case before taking off his gloves and laying them on the top of the safe. Then, with infinite caution, he tugged on the string around his neck and pulled, up out of his shirt collar, the tiny bottle that was suspended from the string. The rubber cork was jammed in tightly and he had to use his teeth to prize it loose. Gently, ever so gently, he poured the contents of the bottle, drop by drop, into the little dam he had made in the clay, so it could run down inside the mechanism of the lock. When it was half empty he stopped and resealed the bottle, then carried it to the far end of the room. He used his handkerchief to wipe the glass free of all fingerprints, then rested the bottle on the wadded-up handkerchief on the floor, tucked neatly into the corner of the floor. The handkerchief had been purchased earlier in the day from an automatic machine.

He sighed, relaxing a bit, when he stood up. He had made it himself, so he knew that it was good nitroglycerine. But it was unreliable stuff at best, and not nice to be around. He put his gloves back on.

There was a rug on the office floor, but it was tacked down and would be too much trouble to try and lift. However the shelves were filled with books; thick tomes, annual reports, weighty, important things. Just what he needed. With silent haste he stripped the shelves, piling the books in a pyramid against the door and sides of the safe. He had left an opening in front of the lock. The very last thing, he slid the tiny metal tube of a detonator into the hole and unrolled the wire across the room. Then he sealed the open space with the thickest of the books.

"*Langsam . . . langsam . . .*" he muttered, and crouched behind the desk. The building was silent. There was a small outlet that he built into the case of the flashlight. The two-pronged plug on the end of the wire fitted neatly into it. Schmidt bent lower and jammed in the plug.

The explosion was a muffled blow that shook the floor. The pile of books began to topple, and he ran to catch them. He stopped most of them, but *Annual Fisheries Report 1948—1949* landed with a resounding thud. Smoke curled up and the lock mechanism was a twisted ruin. With careful speed he began moving the books so the safe door could be opened—then froze as heavy footsteps sounded in the outer office. They came closer, right up to the door, and the handle turned.

"Who is in there? Why is this door locked?"

Schmidt put down the books he was holding and turned off the flashlight, then moved to the door. The tape pulled away soundlessly and the plastic sheet rustled as it fell to the floor. He waited until the knob turned again—then reached out and pulled the locking wedge free.

The door burst open with dramatic suddenness and the large form of the night watchman stumbled through, gun in hand. Before he could bring it up there were two coughing reports and he kept on going, forward, down to sprawl full length on the floor.

Schmidt put the muzzle of the silenced revolver against the back of the man's coat, over his heart, and pulled the trigger a third time. The figure jerked convulsively and was still.

After checking the outer office and hall to make sure the watchman had been alone, Schmidt closed the doors and went back to work. He hummed happily as the safe door swung open and he searched through it, ignoring completely the dead man on the floor beside him.

13

ELSINORE

"Look at that!" Nils said. "Just look at it." He had the early edition of *Berlingske Tidende* propped up against the coffeepot while he sawed away angrily at his breakfast bacon. "I'm just not used to seeing headlines like that in a Danish paper. Shocking. Night watchman killed . . . foreign minister's office burglarized . . . documents missing. It's like reading the American papers."

"I don't see why you mention the States," Martha said. "These things happened right here, not in America. There's no connection." She took the pot to pour herself some coffee, and his newspaper fell down.

"I would appreciate it if you would keep my paper out of the preserves, it makes it hard to read." He picked it up and brushed at the red smears with his napkin. "There is a connection, and you know it. The U.S. papers are always filled with murders, rapes, and beatings because that sort of thing always happens there. What was the figure? There are more murders in the city of Dallas in one year than in all of England, Ireland, Scotland, and Wales combined. And I'll bet you could throw in Denmark too."

"If you hate Americans so much—why did you ever marry me?" Martha asked, biting into her toast.

He opened his mouth to answer, found that there was absolutely nothing he could say to this fine bit of female logic, so he growled instead and opened to the soccer scores. Martha nodded as if this was just the kind of answer that she expected.

"Shouldn't we get going?" she asked.

Nils glanced up at the clock over the kitchen door. "A few minutes more. We don't want to get there before the post office opens at nine." He put the paper down and reached for his coffee. He was wearing a dark brown suit instead of his uniform.

"Won't you be flying any more?" Martha asked.

"I don't know. I would like to, but Skou keeps talking about security. I suppose we had all better start listening a little closer to Skou. You better get your coat now. I'll wait for you in the car."

A door led from the utility room into the garage, which made this bit of deception easier. Skou had agreed that the chances were slim that Nil's home was under surveillance, but one could never be sure. The way Skou talked, he made it seem as though every flight into Denmark had more secret agents than tourists aboard. He might be right at that; there wasn't a country in the world that didn't want the Daleth drive. He opened the back door of the big Jaguar and slid in. His knees crunched up, and he realized that he had never sat in the back seat before. Martha came in, looking chic and attractive in the brown suede coat, a bright silk band on her hair—and a lot younger than her twenty-six years. He rolled the window down.

"Child-bride," he called out. "You never kissed me goodbye."

"I'd cover you with lipstick." She blew him a kiss. "Now close the window and hunker down before I open the garage door."

"Hunker down," he grunted, forcing his massive frame down on the floor. "American. You learn new words every day. Can you hunker up too?"

"Be quiet," she said, getting into the car. "The street looks empty."

They pulled out, and all he could see were the treetops along Strandvejen while she closed the door again. When they started up there was just sky and an occasional cloud.

"Very dull back here."

"We'll be there soon. The train is at nine-twelve, is that right?"

"On the button. Don't get there too early, because I don't feel like standing around the platform."

"I'll go slow through the forest. Will you be home for dinner?"

"No way to say. I'll call you as soon as I know."

"Not before noon. I'll do some shopping while I'm in Birkerod. There's that new little dress shop."

"There's some new little bills." He sighed dramatically and unsuccessfully tried to shift position.

It was nine minutes past nine when she pulled into the parking space next to the railroad station, just across the street from the post office.

"Is there anyone around?" he asked.

"Somebody going into the post office. And a man locking up his bike. He's going into the station, now—no one is looking this way."

Nils pushed up gratefully and dropped into the seat. "A big relief."

"You will be all right, won't you?" she asked, turning about to face him. She had that little worried pucker between her eyes that she used to have when they were first married, before the routine of his flying pushed the concern below the surface.

"I'll be just fine," he assured her, reaching out and rubbing the spot on her forehead with his finger. She smiled, not very successfully.

"I never thought that I would wish you were back at flying those planes all over the world. But I do."

"Don't worry. Little Nils can take care of himself. And watchdog Skou will be with me."

He watched the graceful swing of her figure as she crossed the road—then looked at his watch. One more minute. The street was empty now. He climbed out of the car and went to buy a ticket. When he stepped out on the wooden platform the train was just rounding the bend on the outskirts of town, moaning deeply. There were a few other people waiting for the train from Copenhagen, none of them looking at him. When the coaches squealed to a stop he boarded the first one. Ove Rasmussen looked up from his newspaper and waved. They shook hands and Nils sat down in the empty seat next to him.

"I thought Arnie would be with you," Nils said.

"He's going up with Skou in some other complicated and secret manner."

"It's stopped being a game, hasn't it?"

"You're right about that. I wonder if they'll be able to find the swine who did it?"

"Highly unlikely, Skou told me. Very professional, no clues of any kind. The murdering bastards. Did them no good either. There was nothing about the Daleth drive in the office."

They were silent after that, all the way to Hillerod where they had to change trains. The Helsingor train was ready to leave, a spur line, one track, and just three cars. It rattled off through the beech and birch forests, skirting the backyards of red-roofed white houses where laundry blew in the fresh wind from the Sound. The woods changed to fields and, at Snekkersten, they saw the ocean for the first time, the leaden waters of the Oresund with the green of Sweden on the far side. This was the last stop before Elsinore and they climbed down to find Skou waiting for them. No one else got off the train at the tiny fishing village. Skou walked away without a word and they followed him. The old houses had high hedges, and the street was empty. Around the first corner a Thames panel truck was waiting. KOBENHAVNS ELEKTRISKE ARTIKLER painted on the sides, along with some enthusiastic lightning bolts and a fiercely glowing light bulb. He opened the back for them and they climbed in, making themselves as comfortable as they could on the rolls of heavy wire inside. Skou got into the driver's seat, changed his soft hat for a workman's peaked cap, and drove off.

Skou took the back roads into Helsingor, then skirted the harbor to the *Helsingor Skibsvaerft*. The guard at the gate waved him through and he drove into the shipyard. There were the skeletons of two ships on the ways. Riveting machines hammered, and there was the sudden bite of actinic light as the welders bent to their work. The truck went around to the rear of the offices, out of sight of the rest of the yard.

"We have arrived," Skou announced, throwing wide the back door.

They climbed down and followed Skou into the building and up a flight of stairs. A uniformed policeman saluted them as they came up and opened the door for them. There was the smell of fresh-brewed coffee inside, mixed with rich cigar smoke. Two men were seated with their backs to the door, looking out of the large window that faced onto the shipyard. They stood and turned around when the others entered, Arnie Klein and a tall middle-aged man dressed in a rusty black suit and vest with an old-fashioned gold watch chain across the front. Arnie made the introductions.

"This is Herr Leif Holm, the shipyard manager."

Coffee was produced, which they accepted, and thick, long Jutland cigars, which they refused, although Holm lit one himself and produced an immense cloud of blue smoke that hung below the ceiling.

"There you see it, gentlemen," Holm said, aiming the cigar, like some deadly weapon, out of the window. "On the central ways. Denmark's hope and future."

A rain squall swept across the harbor, first clouding the battlements of Kronborg Slot, Hamlet's castle, then the squat shape of the Swedish Halsingborg ferry. It threw a misty curtain over the red ribs and plates of the ships under construction before vanishing inland. Watery sunlight took its place. They followed Holm's directions, looking at the squat, almost ugly ship that was nearing completion. It was oddly shaped, like an inner tube that had been stretched into an oblong. Bow, stern, and sides were fat and rounded; the superstructure, now being assembled on the deck in prefabricated units, was low and streamlined.

"That's the new hovercraft, isn't it?" Nils asked. "*Vikingepuden*. Being built for the Esbjerg-to-London run. Supposed to be the biggest in the world." He wondered to himself what the raft had to do with Denmark's hope and future.

"You are correct," Holm said. "Plenty of articles in the papers, publicity, bigger than the British Channel ferries. What they do not mention is that we have been working on her around the clock and that some major changes have been incorporated in her design. And when she is launched she will be christened *Galathea*, and will sail uncharted seas just like her namesake. If she does not plumb the deepest of the ocean deeps, perhaps she will have a better head for heights." He laid his finger alongside his nose and winked broadly.

"You don't mean . . . ?"

"I do indeed. The Moon, the planets, the stars—who knows? I understand that the professors here have been preparing her motive power, while we of the shipbuilding industry have not been idle. Major changes have been made in her plans. Internal bracing, hull, airtight hatches, airlocks—I will not bore you with the details. Suffice to say that in a few short weeks the first true spaceship will be launched. *Galathea*."

They looked at her now with a new and eager interest. The rounded hull, impossible in any normal ocean vessel, was the ideal shape for a pressure hull. The lack of clearly marked bow and stern of no importance in space. This rusty, ugly torus was the shape of the future.

"There is another bit of information that you gentlemen should know. All of the operations of the program have been transferred to a new ministry, which will be made public after *Galathea* is launched. The Ministry of Space. I have the honor of being the acting minister, for the time being. It is therefore my pleasurable duty to ask Captain Hansen if he will request a transfer from the Air Force to the Space Force, with equivalent rank, of course, and no loss in benefits or seniority. If he does, his first assignment will be as commanding officer of this magnificent vessel. What do you say, Captain?"

"Of course," Nils said, "of course!" without an instant's hesitation. He did not take his eyes off the ship even when he accepted his friends' congratulations.

* * *

Martha had not been exactly truthful with Nils when she had left him off at the station in Birkerod. She was not going shopping for dresses today but, instead, was keeping an appointment in Copenhagen. It was a small white lie, not telling him about this, one of the very few she had ever told him since they had been married. Seven years, it must be some sort of record. And the foolish part was that there was no reason why she shouldn't tell Nils. It wasn't very important at all.

Guilt, that's all, she thought, stopping for the light, then turning south on Kongevej. *Just my own irrational feelings of guilt*. Clouds were banking up ahead and the first drops of rain splattered on the windshield. Where would the modern world be without Freud to supply a reason for everything? She had been majoring in psychology at Columbia when she had met Nils for the first time. Visiting her parents here in Copenhagen where her father had been stationed. Dr. Charles W. Greene, epidemiologist, big man with the World Health Organization. Welcoming his daughter for her summer vacation, long-limbed, undergraduate, tweed skirts. Parties and friends. A wonderful summer. And Nils Hansen. Big as a mountain and handsome as Apollo in his SAS uniform. An almost elemental force. Laughing and fun; she had been in bed with him almost before she knew he had been making a pass. There was no time to think or even realize what had happened. The funny part was, in a way, that they had been married afterward. His proposal had come as a real surprise. She liked him well enough, he was practically the first man she had ever been to bed with, because other college students hardly counted. At first it had been a little strange, even thinking about marrying someone other than an American, another country and another language. But in so many ways Denmark seemed like the States and her parents were there, Nils and all her friends spoke English. And it had been fun, sort of instant jet set, and they had been married.

Even though she had never been completely sure why he had ever picked her. He could have had any girl that he wanted to crook his finger at—he still had to beat them off at parties. And he had chosen her. Romantic love she told herself, whenever she was feeling upswing, something right out of the *Ladies' Home Journal*. But when the rain set in for weeks at a time and she was alone she had to go see friends, or buy a hat or something, to get away from the depression.

Then she would worry that he had married her because it was that time of life when Danish men got married. And she had been handy. And an American wife has some prestige in Denmark.

The truth was probably somewhere in between these—or took in parts of both. As she grew up she had discovered that nothing was ever as simple as you hoped it might be. Now she was a long-married woman, a homemaker and on the pill, a little bored at times, though not unhappy.

Yet she was still an American citizen—and that, perhaps, was where the guilt came in. If she loved Nil's, as she was sure she did, why had she never taken the step of becoming a Danish citizen? In all truth she never thought much about it, and whenever her thoughts came near the subject she slithered them away in another direction. It would be easy enough to do. She was driving mechanically and realized suddenly that the rain had gotten heavier, that it was covering the glass, and she slowed and turned on the wipers.

Why didn't she do it? Was this a thin lifeline she held to, to her family, her earlier life? A fractional noncommitment that meant she still had some doubt about their marriage? Nonsense! Nils never mentioned it, she couldn't recall their ever even talking about it. Yet still the guilt. She kept her passport up to date, which made her a foreign resident of Denmark, and once a year a smiling detective at the Criminal Police division stamped an extension into it. Perhaps it was the Criminal Police bit that bothered her? No, that was just a government office, it could have been any office and she knew that she would feel the same. Now the American embassy had some question about a detail in her passport and she was going there. And she had not told Nils about it.

With the morning rush hour over the traffic was light, and she was at the embassy before ten. There wasn't a parking place in sight and she finally ended up over two blocks away. The rain had settled down to a steady Danish drizzle, the kind that could last for days. She slipped on her plastic boots—she always kept a pair in the car—and unfolded the umbrella. Too short for a cab ride, too long to walk. Taking a deep breath, she opened the door. The rain drummed on the transparent fabric of the umbrella.

The lobby, as always, was deserted, and the receptionist behind the big desk looked on with the cold detachment of all receptionists while Martha juggled her closed, dripping umbrella and searched through her purse for the piece of paper.

"I have an appointment," she said, unfolding it and shaking out the crumbs of tobacco. "With a Mr. Baxter. It's for ten o'clock."

"Through those doors there, turn left, room number one seventeen. It's down at the end of the hall."

"Thank you."

She tried to shake all of the water off on the mats, but still trailed a spatter of drops across the marble floor. The door to number 117 was wide open, and a gangling man with thick dark-rimmed glasses was bent over the desk, studying a sheet of paper with fierce concentration.

"Mr. Baxter?"

"Yes, please come in. Let me hang up those wet things for you. Quite a day out. I sometimes think that this whole country is ready to float out to sea." He stood the umbrella in his wastebasket and hung up her coat, then closed the door. "Then you are . . . ?"

"Martha Hansen."

"Of course, I was expecting you. Won't you sit here, please."

"It was about my passport," she said, sitting and opening her purse on her lap.

"If I could see it . . ."

She handed it over and watched while he turned the pages, frowning as he attempted to read some of the smudged visas and customs stamps. He made a few notes on a yellow legal pad.

"You sure seem to like traveling, Mrs. Hansen."

"It's my husband, he's an airline pilot. The tickets are practically free so we do get around a lot."

"You're a lucky woman." He closed the passport and looked at her, his eyebrows raised above the glasses' frame.

"Say, isn't your husband Nils Hansen—the Danish pilot? The one we have been reading about."

"Yes. Is there anything wrong with the passport?"

"No, not at all. You really are lucky married to a man like that. Say, is that pendant you're wearing from the Moon? The one that was in all the papers?"

"Yes, would you like to see it?" She slipped the chain over her head and handed it to him. It was an ordinary bit of crystalline volcanic rock, chipped and untrimmed, that was held in a silver cage. A stone from another world.

"I heard that you had been offered five-figure sums for it. You had better take good care." He handed it back. "I wanted your passport just to check. There has been some difficulty with another passport with almost the same number as yours. We have to be sure, you know. Hope you don't mind?"

"No, of course not."

"Sorry to bother you. But you know how it is. This kind of thing would never happen at home. But an American, living abroad, always a lot of paperwork." He tapped the passport on his blotter but made no attempt to return it.

"My home is here," she said, defensively.

"Of course. Figure of speech. After all, your husband is Danish. Even though you are still an American citizen."

He smiled at her, then looked out of the window at the rain. She clasped her hands tightly on top of her purse and did not answer. He turned back, and she realized that the smile was empty, not sympathetic or friendly. Not anything. A prop just like the glasses that gave him that owlish intellectual look.

"You must be a loyal American citizen," he said, "because you have never considered giving up your citzenship even though you are married—seven years, isn't it?—to a citizen of a foreign country. That's true, isn't it?"

"I—I don't think much about these things," she said in a very small voice, wondering as she spoke. Why didn't she tell him to mind his own business? Take her passport and get out of here? Perhaps because he spoke aloud what she had always known and never mentioned to anyone.

"There's nothing to be ashamed of." The smile came on again. "Loyalty to one's country may be old-fashioned, but there is still something fine about it. Don't let anyone tell you different. There is nothing at all wrong in loving your husband, as I'm sure you do, and being married to him—yet still keeping your God-given American citizenship. It's something they can't take away from you, so don't ever give it up." He made his points sternly, tapping the passport on the desk as he did so.

She could think of nothing to answer, so remained silent. He nodded, as though her silence were some kind of consent.

"I see by the papers that your husband actually flew that Daleth-drive ship to the Moon. He must be a brave man."

She had to at least nod agreement to that.

"The world is looking to Denmark now, for leadership in the space race. It's sort of funny that this little country should be ahead of the United States. After all the billions that we have spent and after all the brave men who have died. A lot of Americans don't think that it's fair. After all, it was America that freed this country from the Germans, and it's American money and men and equipment that keeps NATO strong and defends this country against the Russians. Maybe they have a point. The space race is a big thing and little Denmark can't go it alone, don't you agree?"

"I don't know, really. I suppose they can. . . ."

"Can they?" The smile was gone. "The Daleth drive is more than a space drive. It is a power in the world. A power that Russia could reach out a few miles and grab, just like that. You wouldn't like that to happen, would you?"

"Of course not."

"Right. You're an American, a good American. When America has the Daleth drive there will be peace in the world. Now I'll tell you something, and it's confidential so you shouldn't go around mentioning it. The Danes don't see it in the same way. Certain left-wing factions in the government here—after all they *are* socialists—are keeping the Daleth material from us. And we can imagine why, can't we?"

"No," she said defensively. "Denmark isn't like that, the

people in government. They have no particular love for the Russians. There is no need to worry."

"You're a little naïve, like most people, when it comes to international Communism. They are in everywhere. They will get this Daleth drive away from the free world if we don't get it first. You can help us, Martha."

"I can talk to my husband," she said quickly, a cold feeling of dread in her chest. "Not that it would do much good. He makes up his own mind. And I doubt if he can influence anyone . . ." She broke off as Baxter shook his head in a long, slow *no*.

"That is not what I mean. You know all of the people involved. You visit them socially. You have even visited the Atomic Institute—"

"How do you know that?"

"—so you know a good deal more about what is happening than anyone else not formally connected with the project. There are some things I would like to ask you—"

"No," she said breathlessly, jumping to her feet. "I can't do it—what you are asking. It's not fair to ask me. Give me my passport, please, I must go now."

Unsmiling, Baxter dropped the passport into a drawer and closed it. "I'll have to hold this. Just a formality. Check the number against the records. Come back and see me next week. The receptionist will make an appointment." He went to the door ahead of her and put his hand on the knob. "We're in a war, Martha, all over the world. And all of us are front-line soldiers. Some are asked to do more than others, but that is the way wars are. You are an American, Martha—never forget that. You can't ever forget your country or where your loyalties lie."

14

There was something final about cleaning out his locker that depressed Nils. Number 121 in Kastrup airport, it had always been his, no one else's. When they had enlarged this section and built the new lockers he, as Senior Danish Pilot, had of course had first pick. Now he was emptying it. No one had asked him to, but when he had stopped off to pick up the boiler suits he had stowed here, he had realized that he no longer had any right to the locker. In all fairness he should let someone else use it. As quickly as possible he stuffed all the accumulated odds and ends of the years into the flight bag and zipped it shut. The hell with it. He slammed the door shut and stamped out.

In the hallway he suddenly realized that someone was calling his name and he looked about.

"Inger!"

"None other, you big ape. You have been flying too much without me. Isn't it time you hired a good hostess for your Moon trips?"

She strode toward him, long-legged, willowy. A good hostess indeed, a walking advertisement for SAS. Her skirt was short, her jacket round and tight-fitting, her little cap perched at a jaunty angle on her ash-blond hair. She was the tired traveler's dream of a hostess, bigger than life size, almost as tall as Nils, a vision from a Swedish film. And almost incidentally, the best and most experienced hostess the airline had. She took his hand in both of hers, standing very close.

"It's not true, is it?" she asked. "That you're through with flying?"

"I'm through with SAS, at least now. Other things,"

"I know, big hush-hush stuff. This Daleth drive. The

papers are full of it. But I can't believe that we won't ever fly together again!"

As she said it she leaned even closer and he could feel the tall warmth of her against his side, the roundness of her breasts pushing against his arm. Then she leaned back, knowing better than to show anything more in public.

"God, how I wish we could!" he said, and they both laughed aloud at the sudden hoarseness of his voice.

"The next time you are out of the country let me know." She looked at her watch and dropped his hand. "I have to run. A flight out in an hour."

She waved and was gone, and he went the other way. Walking with the memory of her. How many countries had it been? Sixteen, something like that. The very first time she had flown on his crew they had ended up in bed together by mutual and almost automatic decision. It had been New York City in the summer, an exhaust-fumed and sooty inferno just on the other side of the window. But the blinds on the hotel-room window had been closed and the air conditioner hummed coolly and they had explored each other with sweet abandon. There had been no guilt, just a pleasurable acceptance without past or future. He scarcely thought about her when she wasn't present, and neither was jealous of the other. But when they did meet they had a single thought.

It was after a particularly enjoyable night on a singularly lumpy mattress in Karachi that they had first started to figure out how many cities they had made love in. They were exhausted, mostly with laughing, because Nils had bought her a book of photographs of erotic temple carvings. They had tried some of the more exotic postures—the ones that did not need three or four others to help—chortling too much to really accomplish anything. They had lain there afterward and had had a not too serious argument about just how many cities it really had been. After this they began to keep track. Nils then used his seniority to bid for different runs so they could be together, adding new cities to the lengthening list. But never Copenhagen, or even Scandinavia, never at home. There was an entire world out there that they shared. This was his home and it was something different. It was an unspoken rule that they knew about but never discussed. He pushed open the door to the main terminal and growled deep in his throat.

A girl's voice on the public address system announced departing flights in a dozen languages. Danish and English for every flight, then the language of the country of destination: French for the Paris flight, Greek for the Athens plane, even Japanese for the Air Japan polar flight to Tokyo. Nils worked through the crowds to the nearest TV display of arrivals and departures. There was a shuttle flight leaving soon for Malmö, just across the Sound in Sweden, that would do fine. Skou was always finding new ways to elude any possible attempt to follow them, and this was his latest device. A good one too, Nils had to admit.

He waited in the main hall until just two minutes before departure time. Then he went through the administrative part of the building, where passengers were not allowed. This should have shaken any possible tails. A few people greeted him, and then he was out on the tarmac just as the final passengers were boarding the Malmö flight. He was the last one in, and they closed the door behind him. The hostess knew him—he didn't even have to show her his pass—and he went up and sat on the navigator's chair and talked shop with the pilots during the brief hop. When they landed, the hostess let him out first and he went directly to the parking lot. Skou was there, behind the wheel of a new Humber, reading a sports newspaper.

"What happened to that *gamle raslekasse* you always drive?" Nils asked, sliding in next to him.

"Old rattling tin can indeed! It has thousands of kilometers left in it. It happens to be in the garage for a little work . . ."

"Jacking up the steering wheel to build a new car underneath!"

Skou snorted through his nostrils and started the engine, easing out of the lot and heading north.

Once clear of the city, the coast road wound up and down between the villages, revealing quick glimpses of the Sound, on their left, seen through the trees. Skou concentrated on his driving, and Nils had little to say. He was thinking about

Inger, erotic memories, one after another, something new for him. He normally lived the moments of existence as they came, planning only as far ahead as was necessary, forgetting the past as something long gone and unalterable. He missed flying, that was for certain, realizing now that this had been the biggest element of his life around which everything else turned. Yet he had not flown an airplane since . . . when? Before the Moon flight. It seemed that he had been buried in offices and that filthy shipyard for years. The short flight from Kastrup had only teased him. A passenger.

"Here," he called out suddenly. "Let me drive a bit, Skou. You can't have all the fun."

"This is a *government* car!"

"And I'm a government slave. Let's go. I'll report you to your superiors for getting drunk on the job if you don't let me."

"I had one beer with lunch—and a flat Swedish beer at that. I ought to report you for blackmail." But Skou pulled up anyway and they changed seats. He said nothing when Nils put his foot flat on the floor and screamed the engine up through the gears.

There was hardly any traffic on the road and the visibility was good, with the setting sun trying to get through the clouds. The Humber cornered like a sports car, and Nils was an excellent driver, going fast but not taking chances. Machines were something he knew how to cope with.

It was almost dark when they reached Hälsingborg and bumped over the railroad tracks to the ferry terminal. They began a new lane and were the first car aboard the next ferry, stopping right behind the folding gate at the bow of the ship. Skou got on line to buy a package of tax-free cigarettes during the brief crossing, but Nils stayed in the car. The drive, short as it was, had helped. He watched the lights of the castle and the Helsingor harbor come close and thought about the work that was nearing completion on *Galathea*.

The guard at the shipyard gate recognized Skou and waved them through.

"How is security?" Nils asked.

"Secrecy is the best security. So far the spies have not

connected the much-publicized hovercraft with the highly secret Daleth project. So the guards stationed here—and there are enough of them—are not in evidence. You saw one of them, selling hot dogs from that cart across the street."

"The *polsevogn*! Does he get to keep his profits?"

"Certainly not! He's on salary."

They parked in their usual spot behind the buildings, and Nils used the office to change into his boiler suit. The yards were silent, except for the work going on around the *Galathea* which continued on a twenty-four-hour basis. Arc lights had been switched on, lighting up the rusted, unfinished hull. This was deliberate subterfuge: the sandblasting and painting was being put off until the very last moment.

Inside, it was very different. They climbed the ladder and entered through the deck airlock. The lights came on when the outer door was closed. Beyond the inner door stretched a white corridor, linoleum floored, walled with teak paneling. The lighting was indirect and unobtrusive. Framed photographs of the lunar landscape were fastened to the walls.

"Pretty luxurious," Nils said. On his last visit the corridor had been red-painted steel.

"Most of it is from the original specifications," Ove Rasmussen said, coming in behind them. "All of the interior was designed and contracted for. There had to be some changes, of course, but in most of the cabins and general areas there was very little. They filed away the pictures of castles and thatched houses and put up these Moon shots instead. These are the prints the Soviets sent in gratitude. Come with me, I have a surprise for you."

They went along a carpeted passage lined with cabin doors. Ove pointed to the last one and said, "You first, Nils." There was a brass plate let into the teak of the door that read *Kaptajn*. Nils pushed it open.

It was large, part office and part living room, with a bedroom opening off of it. The dark blue carpet was flecked with a pattern of tiny stars. Over the desk, which was an ultra-modern palisander-and-chrome construction, were mounted a bank of instruments and a row of communicators.

"A little different from flying SAS," Ove said, smiling at

Nils's wide-eyed appreciation. "Or even the Air Force. And look there, your first command, in true nautical tradition."

Over the couch was a large color photograph of the little submarine *Blaeksprutten* sitting on the lunar plain. The distant Earth showed clearly in the background.

"Another gift from the Soviets?" Nils laughed. "It's all tremendous."

"Personal present from Major Shavkun. He took it before they came over, you remember. See, all three of them have signed it."

"A little paint on the outside and *Galathea* looks ready to go. Is it? How does the drive department progress?"

"The fusion generator is aboard and has been tested. A lot of small items are still to be taken care of—nothing important, silverware, things like that. And the Daleth drive, of course. It's built and has been bench tested at the institute, and it will go in last."

"The *very* last thing," Skou said. "We want to put as little temptation in the way of our spies as is possible. We have the university under a heavy military guard, so I imagine they are focusing their interest there." He smiled broadly. "All of the hotels are full. They bring in plenty of foreign exchange. It is a new tourist industry."

"And you're in security heaven," Nils said. "No wonder you are driving a new Humber. Where is Arnie Klein?"

"He has been living aboard for the last couple of weeks," Ove said. "Ever since the bench tests were completed on the Daleth unit. He has been working with my fusion generator and, I swear, he has already made at least five patentable improvements."

"Let's get down there. I want to see my engine room." He looked around once more, admiringly, before he closed the door behind them. "All of this takes a bit of getting used to. It is beginning to be a bigger job than I ever realized."

"Relax," Ove told him. "It's a ship now, but it is going to be a big flying machine once you lift off. Sort of a super seven forty-seven—which I know you have flown. You'll agree that it is a lot easier to teach you to fly a ship than it is to teach a ship's captain to fly anything at all."

"There is that— What's wrong?"

Skou had stopped dead, nostrils flared with anger.

"The guard, he should be there in front of the engine-room door. Twenty-four hours a day." He began to run heavily, with a bobbing motion, and pushed against the door. It would not open.

"Locked from the inside," Nils said. "Is there another key?"

Skou was not wasting time looking for a key. He drew a short thick-barreled revolver from a holster inside the waistband of his trousers and jammed it against the lock. It boomed once and jumped in his hand. Smoke billowed out and the door opened. Just a few centimeters, something was blocking it. Through the opening they could see the blue-clad legs of the guard on the floor just inside, his body pressing against the door. He slid along, unprotesting, when they pushed harder to get the door open.

"Professor Klein," Skou called, and jumped in over the guard's body. Three rapid shots boomed out and he kept on going, falling to the floor. He had his gun raised but did not return the fire. "Stay back," he called to the other two, then climbed to his feet.

Ove hesitated but Nils dived in, rolling over the guard without touching him. He sat up just in time to see a flicker of motion as the large engine-room airlock closed. He scrambled up, ran to it and pulled strongly but it would not budge.

"Dogged shut from the other side! Where is Arnie?"

"With them. I saw him. Two men, carrying him. Both armed. Damn!" Skou had his pocket radio out, switched on, but nothing except static was coming from it.

"Your radio won't work in here," Ove reminded him, bending over the guard. "You're surrounded by metal. Get up on deck. This man is just unconscious, he's been hit by something."

The other two were past him and gone. There was nothing he could do now for the guard. Ove jumped to his feet and ran after them.

Both airlock doors were open and Skou, on the deck outside, was shouting into his radio. The results were almost instantaneous: he had been prepared for this emergency too.

All of the shipyard lights came on at once, including searchlights on the walls and the arcs mounted on the cranes and ships under construction. The yard was as light as day. Sirens sounded out in the harbor and searchlights played over the black water as two police boats sealed off that side. Nils scrambled down the ladder and jumped the last few meters to the ground, hit running, around the turn of the hull to the stern where the airlock was. The outer door gaped open and he had a quick glimpse of dark figures. He grabbed the arm of a policeman who ran heavily up.

"Do you have a radio? Fine. Call Skou. Tell him they have headed toward the water. They probably have a boat. *Hold your fire*. There are two men. They are carrying Professor Klein. We can't risk hurting him." The policeman nodded agreement, pulling out his radio, and Nils ran on.

The shipyard was a bedlam. Workers ran for cover while police cars careened in through the gate, horns shrieking. Skou passed on Nils's message in breathless spurts as he ran. There were guards ahead of him, converging on the waterfront and the slipway, where the ribs of a ship under construction stretched rusty fingers toward the sky.

Red flame spurted from behind a stack of hull plates and a guard folded, his hands over his midriff, and collapsed. The others sought cover, raising their guns.

"Don't shoot!" Skou ordered, going on alone. "Get some lights over there."

Someone swung a heavy arc light around, following the direction of the spotlight on one of the police cars. It burned, bright as daylight, on the spot. Skou ran on, crookedly, alone.

A man, all in black, stood up, shielding his eyes, raising a long-barreled pistol. He fired once, twice, a bullet hit his coat. Skou stopped, raised his own pistol into the air and lowered it slowly onto the target, calm as though he were on the pistol range. The invader fired again and Skou's gun cracked out almost at the same instant, a single shot.

The man jerked, spun about and dropped onto the steel plates, the weapon rattling from his grasp. Skou signaled two of the policemen to examine him and hobbled on, ignoring the huddled shape. A line of guards and police closed in behind him; a patrol boat moved closer to shore, its motor rumbling and its spotlight sweeping the deep shadows of the ways.

"There they are!" someone shouted as the spotlight ceased shifting and came to rest. Skou stopped, and halted the others with a signal.

The riveted plates of the keel were a stage, the curved ribs a proscenium, the scene was lit. The drama was one of life and death. A man in shining black from head to toe half crouched behind Arnie Klein's slumped form. He supported Arnie with an arm across his chest. His other hand held a gun, the muzzle of which was pressed against Arnie's head. The sirens died, their work done, the alarm given, and a sudden silence fell. In it the man's voice was loud and hoarse, his words clear.

"Don't come here—I kill!"

The words were in English, thickly accented but understandable. There were no movements from the onlookers as he began to drag Arnie's limp form along the keel toward the water's edge.

Nils Hansen stepped from the shadows behind him and reached out a great hand that engulfed the other's, trapping it, pulling the gun into the air and away from Arnie's head. The man in black shrieked, in pain or surprise, and the pistol fired, the bullet vanishing into the darkness.

With his free hand Nils pulled Arnie from the other's grasp, and slowly and carefully bent to lay him on the steel plate below. The man he held captive writhed ineffectually against his grip, then began beating at Nils with his fist. Nils ignored him until he straightened up again, seemingly ignorant of the blows striking him. Only then did he reach out and pluck the gun from the other's grasp and hurl it away. And draw his hand back, to bring it down in a quick, open-palmed slap. The man spun half around, dropped, hanging from Nil's unrelenting grasp.

"I want to talk to him!" Skou shouted, hurrying up.

Nils now had the man in both hands, shaking him like a great doll, holding him out to Skou. He was dressed in rubberized black, a frogman's suit, and only his head was uncovered. His skin was sallow, with a thin moustache drawn like a black pencil line on his upper lip. One cheek flared red with the print of a great hand.

For a brief moment the man struggled in Nil's unbreakable grip, looking at the approaching policemen. Then he stopped, realizing perhaps that there was no escape. There was no more resistance in him. He lifted his hand and chewed his thumbnail, a seemingly infantile gesture.

"Stop him!" Shouting, trying to hurry. Too late.

A look of shock, passed over the man's face. His eyes widened and his mouth opened in a soundless scream. He writhed in Nils's hands, his back arching, more and more, impossibly, until he collapsed limply, completely.

"Let him go," Skou said, peeling open one eyelid. "He's dead. Poison in the nail."

"The other one too," a policeman said. "You shot him in . . ."

"I know where I shot him."

Nils bent over Arnie, who was stirring, rolling his head with his eyes closed. There was a red welt behind his ear, already swollen.

"He seems to be all right," Nils said, looking up. He caught sight of the blood on Skou's pants leg and shoe, dribbling onto the metal plate. "You're hurt!"

"The same leg they always shoot me in. My target leg. It doesn't matter. It is more important to get the Professor to the hospital. What a mess. They've found us, someone. It is going to get much worse from now on."

15

Sitting in the darkness, on his bridge, in his chair, Nils Hansen tried to picture himself operating these controls of the *Galathea*. Normally not a very imaginative man, he could, when he had to, visualize how a machine would operate, how it would behave. He had test piloted almost all the new jets purchased by SAS, as well as tested new and experimental planes for the Air Force. Before flying a plane he would study blueprints and construction, sit in a mock-up for simulated flight, talk to the engineers. He would learn all the intricacies of the craft he was to fly, learn everything that he possibly could before that moment when he was committed, he alone, to taking it into the air. He was never bored, never in a hurry. Others grew exasperated at his insistence upon examining every little detail, but he never did. Once airborne he was on his own. The more knowledge he carried aloft with him, the better chance he had of a successful flight—and of returning alive.

Now, his particular powers had been taxed to their limit. This craft was so impossibly big, the principles were so new. Yet he had flown ***Blaeksprutten***, and that experience was the most valuable of all. Remembering the problems, he had worked along with the engineers in laying out the controls and instrumentation. Reaching out he touched the wheel lightly—the same standard wheel, purchased from stock, that was in a Boeing 707 jet. He almost felt right at home. This was connected through the computer to the Daleth drive and would be used for precision maneuvers such as take-off and landing, Altimeter, air-speed indicator, true-speed read-out, power consumption—his eyes moved from one to the other, unerringly, despite the darkness.

There was a large pressure-sealed glass port set into the

steel wall before him that now gave a good view of the shipyard and the harbor. Although it was after two in the morning and Helsingor was long asleep, the area on all sides of the shipyard was brightly lit and astir with movement. Police cars cruised slowly along the waterfront and flashed their lights into the narrow side streets. A squad of soldiers moved in loose formation among the buildings. Extra spotlights were mounted above the normal streetlights so the entire area was bright as day. The motor torpedo boat *Hejren* was anchored across the near end of the harbor with its gun turrets manned and trained.

There was the hum of motors as the bridge door slid open and the radio operator came in, going to his position. Skou was behind him, hobbling on a single crutch. He stood for a moment next to Nils, eyes moving over his posted defenses outside. With a grunt, possibly of approval, he dropped into the second pilot's chair.

"They know we're here," he said. "But that's all they are going to know. How is this tub?"

"Checked, double-checked, and a few times after that. I've done what I can, and the engineers and inspectors have been over every inch of hull and every piece of equipment. Here are their signed reports." He held up a thick folder of papers. "Anything new on last week's visitors?"

"A blank, all along the line. Frogman equipment bought right here, in Copenhagen. No marks, tags, papers. Their guns were German P-thirty-eights, Second World War vintage. Could have come from anyplace. We thought we had a lead on their fingerprints, but it was a mistaken identification. I checked it myself. Nothing. Two invisible men from nowhere."

"Then you'll never know what country sent them?"

"I don't really care. A wink is as good as a nod. Someone has winked us and, after that dust-up, the whole world knows that there is something going on up here. They just don't know what, and I've kept them far enough away so they can't learn more." He leaned forward to read the glowing dial of the clock. "Not too much longer to go. Everything set?"

"All stations manned, ready to go when they give the word. Except for Henning Wilhelmsen. He's lying down or sleeping until I call him. It's his job tonight."

"Better do that now."

Nils took up the phone and dialed Henning's number; it was answered instantly.

"Commander Wilhelmsen here."

"Bridge. Will you report now."

"On the way!"

"There!" Skou said, pointing to the road at the far end of the harbor where a half-dozen soldiers on motorcycles had appeared. "It's moving like clockwork—and well it better! She has been staying at Fredensborg Castle, twenty minutes away."

Two open trucks, filled with soldiers, came behind the motorcycles, then more motorcycles acting as outriders to a long, black, and exceedingly well-polished Rolls Royce. More soldiers followed. As though this appearance had been a signal—and it undoubtedly was—truckloads of troops streamed out of the barracks of Kronborg Castle, where they had been waiting in readiness. By the time the convoy and the car they guarded had reached the entrance to the shipyard, a solid cordon of troops surrounded it.

"What about the lights in here?" Nils asked.

"You can have them on now. It's obvious to the whole town now that something is up."

Nils switched on the ultraviolet control-board illumination so that all the instruments glowed coldly. Skou rubbed his hands together and smiled. "It's all working by clockwork. Notice—I command no one. All has been arranged. Every spy-tourist in town is trying to see what is happening, but they can't get close. In a little while they will be trying to send messages and to leave and will be even less successful. Good Danes are in bed at this hour, they'll not be disturbed. But all the roads are closed, the trains are not running, the phones don't work. Even the bicycle paths are sealed. Every road and track—even the paths through the woods—are guarded."

"Do you have hawks standing by to catch any carrier pigeons?" Nils asked innocently.

"No! By God, should I?" Skou looked worried and chewed at his lip until he saw Nils's smile. "You're only kidding. You shouldn't do that. I'm an old man and who knows, poof, my ticker could stop at a sudden shock."

"You'll outlive us all," Henning Wilhelmsen said, coming onto the bridge. He was wearing his best uniform, cap and all, and he saluted Nils. "Reporting for duty, sir."

"Yes, of course," Nils said, and groped under the control panel for his own hat. "Throw Dick Tracy out of your chair there and we'll get started on the pre-launch checklist."

He found the cap and put it on; he felt uncomfortable. He took it off and looked at the dimly seen emblem on the front, the new one with the *Daleth* symbol on a field of stars. With a quick motion he threw the cap back under the controls.

"Remove your cap," he said firmly. "No caps to be worn on the bridge."

Skou stopped at the door and called back. "And thus the first great tradition of the Space Force is born."

"And no civilians on the bridge, either!" Nils called after the retreating, chuckling figure.

They ran through the list, which ended with calling the crew to their stations. Henning switched on the PA system, and his voice boomed the command in every compartment of the ship. Nils looked out of the port, his attention caught by a sudden bustle below. A fork lift was pushing out a prefabricated wooden platform, ready draped with bunting. It was halted just at the curve of the bow and secured in position; men, dragging wires, ran up the stairs on its rear. Everything was still going according to schedule. The phone rang and Henning answered it.

"They're ready with that patch from the microphones now," he told Nils.

"Tell them to stand by. Hook it into the PA after you have made an alert check on all stations."

The crew was waiting, ready at their stations. They were checked, one by one, while Nils watched the crowd of notables come forward. A military band had appeared and was playing gustily; a thin thread of the music could be heard even through the sealed hull. The crowd parted at the stand

and a tall brown-haired woman made her way up the stairs first.

"The Crown Princess Margrethe," Nils said. "You better get that patch connected."

The small platform was soon filled, and the PA system came on in the middle of an official speech. It was astonishingly short—Skou's security regulations must have ordered that—and the band struck up again. Her Royal Highness stepped forward as one of the crewmen on deck lowered a line to the platform, a bottle of champagne dangling from the end. The Princess's voice was clear, the words were simple.

"I christen thee *Galathea*. . . ."

The sharp crash of the bottle against the steel hull was clearly heard. Unlike an ordinary christening the ship was not launched at once. The officials moved back to a prepared position and the platform was dragged clear. Only then were the launching orders given. The retaining blocks were knocked clear, and a sudden shudder passed through the ship.

"All compartments," Nils said into the microphone. "See that your loose equipment is secured as instructed. Now take care of yourselves, because there is going to be a slam when we hit the water."

They moved, faster and faster, the dark water rushing toward them. A tremor, more of a lifting surge than a shock, ran through the fabric of the ship as they struck the water. They were slowed and stopped by the weight of the chain drags, then rocked a bit in the waves caused by their own launching. The tugs and service boats closed in.

"Done!" Nils said, relaxing his hands from their tight grip on the edge of the control panel. "Is the launching always this hard on one?"

"Never!" Henning answered. "Most ships aren't more than half-finished when they are launched—and I have never heard of one being launched that was not only ready to cruise but had an entire crew aboard. It's a little shocking."

"Unusual times cause unusual circumstances," Nils said calmly, now that the tension of the launching was over. "Take the wheel. As long as we are seaborne you're in command. But don't take her down like you would one of your subs."

"We cruised on the surface most of the time!" Henning was proud of his seamanship. "Plug me into the command circuit," he called to the radio operator.

While Henning made sure that all of the launching supports had been towed free and that the tugs were in position, Nils checked the stations. There had been no damage, they were not shipping water. They were ready to go.

They could have moved under their own power, but it had been decided that the tugs should warp them free of the harbor first. No one knew what kind of handling characteristics this unorthodox ship would have, so the engines would not be started until they were in the unobstructed waters of the Sound. After a brief exchange of sharp, fussy blasts on their whistles, the tugs got under way. As they moved slowly down the harbor, following the torpedo boat that had weighed anchor and preceded them, they had their first clear sight of the area beyond.

"Some secret launching," Henning said, pointing at the crowds that lined the seawall. They were cheering, waving their arms, and the bright patches of Danish flags were to be seen everywhere.

"Everyone in town knew that something was up here. Once we were launched you couldn't stop them from turning out."

The tugs swung a long arc and headed for the harbor entrance. The mole and seawall on either side were black with people, and still more running toward the entrance. As the ship slipped through they waved and shouted, many of them with coats over pajamas, wearing a motley array of fur hats, raincoats, anoraks, anything that could be thrown on quickly. Nils resisted a strong impulse to wave back. Then they were through, away from the lights, into the waters of the Oresund: the first waves broke over the low decks, washing around the boots of the crewmen who tended the lines there.

Well clear of the shore the tugs cast off, tooted farewell, and turned about.

"Cast off," Henning said. "Decks cleared and hatches secured."

"You may proceed then," Nils said.

There were a separate set of controls at the second pilot's position, used only for surface navigation. Two great electric motors were mounted on pods secured to the hull of the ship. Only electric cables penetrated the pressure hull, assuring an airtight continuity. Each motor drove a large six-bladed propeller. There was no rudder; steering was controlled by varying the relative speed of the propellers, which could even be run in opposite directions for sharp turning. Throttles and steering were all controlled from the single position on the bridge, accurate and smooth control being assured by the computer, which monitored the entire operation.

Henning eased forward both throttles and *Galathea* came to life. No longer shorebound, no longer at tow, she was a vessel in her own right. Waves broke against the bow, streamed down the sides, then splashed onto the deck as their speed increased. The lights of Helsingor began to fall behind them. A dash of spray hit the port.

"What's our speed?" Nils asked.

"A stupendous six knots. Our hull has all the fine seagoing characteristics of a gravy boat."

"This will be her first and last ocean cruise, so relax." He made a quick calculation. "Slacken off to five knots, that will get us to the harbor at dawn."

"Aye aye, sir."

Their maiden voyage was going more smoothly than anyone had expected. There was some water seepage around one of the hatches, but this was caused by an incorrectly sized gasket and they could fit one of the spares as soon as they docked. In the semidarkness of the bridge Nils crossed his fingers: it should only stay this way.

"Do you want some coffee, Captain?" Henning asked. "I had some made and put in thermos bottles before we shut the kitchen down."

"A good idea—send for it."

A tall seaman, sporting sidewhiskers and a great moustache, brought it a few minutes later, stamping in in his heavy sea boots and saluting broadly.

"Who the devil are you?" Nils asked. He had never seen the man before.

"He's one of the extra deckhands you asked me to get," Henning answered. "They had to be found and cleared, three of them, and they just came aboard this afternoon. Things were pretty busy at the time. Jens here has been trying to volunteer for this assignment for months. He says he has experience with the Daleth drive."

"You what?"

"Yes sir, Captain. I helped weld up the first experimental one. Nearly broke the back of our ship, it did. Captain Hougaard is still trying to find someone to sue."

"Well—glad to have you aboard, Jens," Nils said, feeling self-conscious about the nautical terms, though no one else seemed to notice.

Their slow voyage continued. It was less than thirty kilometers by sea from Helsingor to Copenhagen, and it was taking them longer than the million-kilometer voyage to the Moon. They had no choice. Until the Daleth drive was installed, they were nothing more than an underpowered electric tub.

The eastern horizon was gold-barred with dawn when they came to the entrance to the Free Port of Copenhagen. Two tugs, riding the easy swell, were waiting for them. They tied up and, in a reverse of their leavetaking, were eased gently into the Frihavn, to the waiting slip at the Vestbassin.

"That's good timing," Nils said, pointing to the convoy just pulling up on the wharf. "They must have been tracking us all the time. Skou told me he had almost a full division of soldiers deployed here. Lining the streets every foot of the way from the Institute. I wish it were all over." He clenched and unclenched his fists, the only sign of tension.

"You and I both. Nothing can go wrong. Too many precautions, but still . . ."

"Still, all of our eggs are in one basket. There is the drive." He pointed to the plastic-wrapped bulk already being eased from the flatbed truck by the dockside crane. "And the professors will be right there with it. All in one basket. But don't worry, it looks like the entire Danish army is out there. Nothing short of an atom bomb could do anything here today."

"And what is to stop that?" Henning's face was white, strained. "There are a lot of them in this world, aren't there? What is to stop someone who can't get the drive from arranging it so no one can get it? Balance of power . . ."

"Shut up. You have too much imagination." Nils meant to say it kindly, but there was an unexpected harsh edge to his words. They both looked up, starting slightly as a flight of jets, bright in the rising sun, screeched by close overhead.

"Ours," Nils said, smiling.

"I wish they would hurry," Henning answered, refusing to be cheered up.

It would take precision work to get the giant Daleth drive swung aboard and mounted, so despite all the advance preparations it seemed to be maddeningly slow. Even as *Galathea* was being securely moored to the dock, the large hatch on the stern deck was being unbolted and opened; a large crane bent its steel neck over, ready to lift when it was free. The hatch would be used once only, then welded shut. The great steel plate moved up, turning slowly, and was pulled back to the shore. The moment it was free the other crane was swinging out the tubular bulk of the Daleth drive. Carefully, with measured movements, it vanished through the hatchway.

The phone rang and Nils answered it, listening and nodding. "Right. Take him to my cabin, I'll see him there." He hung up and ignored Henning's lifted eyebrows. "Take over, I won't be long."

An officer in the uniform of *Livgarden*, the Royal Life Guards, was waiting when he came. The man saluted and held out a thick cream envelope that had been sealed with red wax. Nils recognized the cypher that had been pressed into the wax.

"I'm to wait for an answer," the officer said.

Nils nodded and tore the envelope open. He read the brief message, then went to his desk. In a holder there was some official ship's stationery, unused until now, that some efficient supply officer had had printed. He took a sheet—this was a fitting first message—and wrote a quick note. He sealed it into an envelope and handed it to the officer.

"I suppose there is no need to address the envelope?" he asked.

"No, sir." The man smiled. "For my own part, for everyone, let me wish you the best of luck. I don't think you have any idea of what the country is feeling today."

"I think that I am beginning to understand." They saluted—and shook hands.

Back on the bridge, Nils thought of the letter resting now in his safe.

"I suppose that you are not going to tell me?" Henning asked.

"No reason why I should." He winked, then called over to the radioman, the only other person on the bridge. "Neergaard, take a break. I want you back in fifteen minutes."

There was silence until the door had soughed shut.

"It was from the King," Nils said. "The public ceremony for this afternoon was a fake all along. A coverup. They are going to announce it, we are supposed to tie up by Amalienborg Palace—but we are not going to. As soon as we are ready we get out of here—and leave. He wished us luck. Sorry he couldn't be here. Once out of the harbor, the next step will be . . ."

"The Moon!" Henning said, looking out at the welders working on the deck.

16

Martha Hansen had trouble sleeping. It wasn't being alone in the empty house that bothered her—that had become a commonplace when Nils was flying. Perhaps she was just too used to having him around the house of late, so that the big double bed seemed empty now that he was gone.

It wasn't that either. Something very important, perhaps dangerous, was happening, and he had not been able to talk to her about it. After all these years she knew him well enough to tell when he was concealing something. Overnight, maybe a few days, he had said, then turned away and switched on the television. It was much more than that, she knew, and the knowledge was keeping her awake. She had dozed off, woken up with a start, and been unable to sleep again after that. Too tired to read, she was too tense to sleep as well, and just tossed and punched her pillow until dawn. Then she gave up. After filling the electric percolator she went and took a shower.

Sipping at the too-hot coffee she tried to find some news on the radio, but there was nothing. Switching to the short wave band she ran through an incomprehensible lecture in some guttural language, flipped past some Arabic minor key music, and finally found the news on the BBC World Service. There was a report on the continuing stalemate in the Southeast Asia talks, and she poured more coffee—almost dropping the cup when she heard *Copenhagen*.

". . . incomplete reports, although no official statements have been made at this time. However eyewitness observers say that the city is filled with troops, and there is a great deal of activity along the waterfront. Unofficial reports link the Nils Bohr Institute, and speculation is rife that further tests of the so-called Daleth drive may now be in progress."

She turned the volume all the way up so she could hear it while she was dressing. What was happening? And, more important, the question she tried to avoid all the time now, how dangerous was it? Since the spies had been killed and Arnie had been hurt she was in continual anticipation of something even worse happening.

Fully dressed, with her gloves on and her car keys already out, she stopped at the doorway. Where was she going and what was she doing? This almost hysterical rushing about suddenly struck her as being foolish in the extreme. It couldn't help Nils in any way. Dropping into a chair in the hall she fought back the strong impulse to burst into tears. The radio still boomed.

". . . and a report just in indicates that the experimental ship, often referred to as a hovercraft, is no longer at the shipyards in Elsinore. It can be speculated that there is some connection between this and the earlier events in Copenhagen. . . ."

Martha slammed the door behind her and opened the garage. There was nothing she could do, she knew that, but she did not have to stay at home. Speeding south on Strandvejen—the road was almost deserted at this hour—she felt that she was somehow doing the right thing.

It did not seem that clear once she reached Copenhagen, a maze of closed streets and soldiers with slung rifles. They were very polite, but they would not let her through. Nevertheless she kept trying, probing around the area in the growing traffic, discovering that a great ring seemed to be thrown around the Free Port area. Once she realized this, she swung wide, through the narrow back streets, and headed for the waterfront again on the other side of Kastellet, the five-sided moated castle that formed the southern flank of the harbor. A block from the waterfront she found a place and parked the car. People passed her on foot, and she could see more of them ahead near the water's edge.

The wind from the Sound pulled the heat from her body, and there was no way to hide from it. More and more people arrived, and the air was alive with rumors as everyone searched the Oresund before them for sign of any unusual activity. Some of the spectators had brought radios, but there were no news reports that mentioned the mysterious events in the Frihavn.

One hour passed, and a second, and Martha began to wonder what she was doing here. She was chilled to the bone. The radios blared, and a sudden chorus of shushing went up from the groups around these radios. Martha tried to get closer, but could not. But she could still make out the gist of the Danish announcement.

The *Galathea* . . . an official launching . . . ceremony . . . Amalienborg Palace in the afternoon . . . There was more, but that was enough. Tired and chilled, she turned to go back to the car. She was certain to be invited to anything public, official. They were probably trying to call her now. Better nap first, then call Ulla Rasmussen to find out what they would be wearing.

A man stood before her, blocking her way.

"You're up early, Martha," Bob Baxter said. "This must be an important day for you." He smiled when he said it, but neither the words nor the smile were real. This was no coincidence, she realized.

"You followed me here. You have been watching my home!"

"The street's no place to talk—and you look cold. Why don't we go into this restaurant here? Get some coffee, a bite of breakfast."

"I'm going home," she said, starting around him. He blocked her with his arm.

"You didn't keep that appointment with me. Passport matters can be serious. Now—what do you say we keep this unofficial and sit down for a cup of coffee together? Can't be anything wrong with that?"

"No." She was suddenly very tired. There was no point in irritating the man. A hot cup of coffee would taste good right now. She allowed him to take her arm and open the door of the café.

They sat by the window, with a view of the Sound over the roofs of the parked cars. The heat felt good, and she kept her coat on. He draped his over the back of the chair and ordered coffee from the waitress, who understood his English. He did not speak again until she brought the coffee and was out of earshot.

"You have been thinking about what I asked you," Baxter said, without any preamble. She looked into the coffee cup when she answered.

"To tell the truth, no. There's nothing, really, that I can do to help you."

"I'm the best judge of that. But you would like to help, wouldn't you, Martha?"

"I would like to, of course, but . . ."

"Now that is much more reasonable." She felt trapped by her words: a generalization suddenly turned into a specific promise. "There are no 'buts' to it. And nothing very hard or different for you to do. You have been friendly with Professor Rasmussen's wife, Ulla, lately. Continue that friendship."

"You *have* been watching me, haven't you?"

He brushed the question aside with his hand as not worth answering. "And you know Arnie Klein as well. He's been to your home a few times. Get to know him better too. He's a key man in this business."

"Do you want me to sleep with him too?" she asked, in a sudden surge of anger at herself, this man, the things that were happening. He did not get angry at her, though his face drew up in stern, disapproving lines.

"People have done a lot worse for their country. People have died for our country. I've devoted my life to this work and I have seen them die. So please keep your dirty little Mata Hari jokes to yourself. Or do you want to make jokes about the boys who got tortured and killed fighting the Japs, Koreans, Charley, all of them? Died making the world safe so you could be a free American and live where you like and do what you like. Free. You do believe in America, don't you?"

He brought the challenge out like an oath, laid down on the table between them, waiting to be picked up and sworn to.

"Of course," she finally said, "but . . ."

"There are no *buts* in loyalty. Like honor it is indivisible.

You know that your country needs you and you make a free choice. There is no need to take your passport away or coerce you in the many possible ways—"

No? she thought, nastily. *Then why mention it at all*?

". . . since you are an intelligent woman. You will do nothing dishonorable, I can guarantee that. You will help to right a wrong."

His voice was drowned out as a flight of jet planes tore by low overhead, and he turned his head quickly to look at them. He pointed after them, with a brief, twisted smile.

"Ours," he said. "Do you know what a jet plane costs? We gave them to Denmark. And guns and tanks and ships and all the rest. Do you know that our country paid *fifty percent* of all the costs to re-arm the Danes after the war? Oh yes we did, though it is kind of forgotten now. Not that we expected gratitude. Though a little loyalty wouldn't have hurt. Instead, I am afraid that we have a good deal of selfishness. What can tiny *Denmark* do in this modern world?" He drawled the word with more than a little contempt. "They can just be greedy and forget their responsibilities and forget that nothing stays secret very long in these times. Remember the Red spies and the atom bomb? Their spies are at work here, right now. They'll get the Daleth drive. And when they do—that's the end of the world as we know it. We're going to be dead, or in chains, and that's all there will be to it."

"It doesn't have to be like that."

"No—because you are going to help. America has been the single bastion of the defense of the free world before, and we are not ashamed to take that rôle again. We can guarantee peace."

Like Vietnam, Laos, Guatemala, she thought, but was too ashamed to say it aloud.

The jets swept by again, circling far out in the Sound. Baxter sipped some of his coffee, then looked at his watch.

"I suppose you will want to go home now and get ready. I imagine that you are invited to the big affair this afternoon for the *Galathea* ship. Your husband must be connected with this project. What does he do?"

There it was, a question she could answer: he must know that from the stricken expression on her face. The silence lengthened.

"Come on, Martha," he said, lightly. "You're not siding with *these* people."

It was said more in humor than in insult, as though the thought were unthinkable: siding with the Devil instead of God.

"He is captain of the ship," she said, almost without thinking, choosing the right side. Only afterward did she tell herself that it would be common knowledge soon, everyone would know it. But not now. Now she had taken a stand.

Baxter did not gloat; he just nodded his head as though what she said was right and natural. He looked out of the window and she saw him start, the first sign of real emotion he had ever expressed. She turned to follow his gaze and found herself suddenly cold, colder than she had been standing outside.

"That's the *Galathea*," he said, pointing to the squat shape that had appeared in the Sound outside. She nodded, staring at it. "Good, there's no point in your lying now. We know some things too. We have high altitude pix of this baby. It was in Elsinore last night, came down here for something, probably the Daleth drive, now going to tie up near the castle. You'll get a closer look at her later. Probably go aboard." He turned his head to stare unwinkingly at her, conveying a message, ***You know what to do if that does happen***. It was she who turned away. She was compromised, she knew; she had drawn sides.

She was not exactly sure how it happened.

The jets screamed low again and there were torpedo boats now visible, boxing in the *Galathea* while she wallowed through the low waves. Ungainly.

"Stopping," Baxter said. "I wonder why, trouble . . ."Then his eyes widened and he half rose from his chair. "No! They're not going to!"

They were. The torpedo boats drew back and the jets thundered away into the distance.

And light as a balloon the *Galathea* rose from the water. For only a moment she hung there, free of the sea, invisibly borne, then moved upward, faster and faster, accelerating, a vanishing blur that disappeared almost instantly in the clouds.

Martha took her handkerchief out, not knowing whether she wanted to laugh or cry, crumpling it in her hands.

"You see." His voice was contemptuous and seemed to come from a great distance. "They even lie to you. The whole affair with the King was a lie. They are running away, trying tricks."

She stood and left, not wanting to hear any more.

17

MOON BASE

"I really cannot do it," Arnie said. "There are a number of other people who can do the job just as well, far better in fact. Professor Rasmussen here, for one. He knows everything about the work."

Ove Rasmussen shook his head. "I would if I could, Arnie. But you are the only one who can say what must be said. In fact I'm the one who suggested that you speak ."

Arnie was surprised at this, and his eyes almost accused Ove of betrayal. But he said nothing about it. He turned instead to the efficient young man from the Ministry of State who had come to the Moon to arrange all the details.

"I have never spoken on television before," Arnie told him. "Nor am I equipped to lie in public."

"No one would ever ask you to lie, Professor Klein," the efficient young man said, snapping open his attaché case and slipping out a folder. "We are asking you to tell only the truth. Someone else will discuss the situation here, tell all the details, and not lie at all. The most that will be said—or not said—will be an error of omission. The work here at Manebasen is not completely finished, and it is no grave crime to suggest that it is. This ship is part of the base now, there are depots outside for the equipment, and construction continues right around the clock."

"He's right," Ove said quietly. "The situation is getting worse all the time in Denmark. There was an attack on the atomic institute last night. A car full of men dressed like police. They broke in, shot it out with the troops when they were discovered. Fourteen dead in all."

"Like Israel—the terror raids," Arnie said, mostly to himself, his eyes mirroring a long-remembered pain.

"Not the same at all," Ove insisted quickly. "You can't hold yourself to blame at all for anything that has happened. But you *can* help stop any further trouble, you realize that?"

Arnie nodded, silently, looking out of the lounge window. The pitted lunar plain stretched away from the ship, but the view of most of the sky was cut off by the sharply rising lip of a large crater. Closer in, a large yellow diesel tractor was digging an immense gouge in the soil, its blue cloud of exhaust vanishing into the vacuum at almost the same instant it appeared. A nest of six large oxygen cylinders was strapped behind the driver.

"Yes, I will do it," Arnie said, and once the decision had been made he dismissed it from his mind. He pointed at the tractor driver, who was dressed in a black and yellow suit with a bubble helmet.

"Any more troubles with suit leaks?" he asked as the State Ministry man hurried out.

"Little ones, but we watch and keep them patched. We're keeping the suit pressure at five pounds, so there is no real trouble. We should be happy we could get pressure suits at all. I don't know what we would have done if we hadn't been able to buy these from the British, surplus from their scotched space program. Once things are settled the Americans and the Soviets will be falling over each other to supply us with suits for—what is the expression?"

"A piece of the action."

"Right. We'll soon have this base dug in and completely roofed over, and we'll convert everything to electrical operation so we won't have to keep bringing oxygen cylinders from Earth."

He broke off as the television crews wheeled in their equipment. Lights and cameras were quickly mounted, the microphone cords spread across the floor. The director, a busy man with a pointed beard and dark glasses, shouted instructions continually.

"Could I ask you boys to move," he said to Ove and Arnie, and waved the prop men toward their chairs. The furniture was shoved aside and rearranged, a long table moved over, while the director framed the scene in his hands.

"I want that window off to one side, the speakers below it, mikes on the table, get a carafe of water and some glasses, find something for that blank hunk of wall." He spun on his heel and pointed "There. That picture of the Moon. Move it over here."

"It's bolted down," someone complained.

"Well unbolt it! That's what you have fat fingers and a little tool kit for." He ran back and looked through the viewer on the camera.

Leif Holm stamped into the room, large as life, wearing the same ancient-cut suit that he had worn in his office in Helsingor.

"Some flight I had in that little *Blaekspruttem*," he said, shaking hands firmly with the two physicists. "If I was a Catholic I would have been crossing myself all the way. Couldn't even smoke. Nils was afraid I would clog up the air equipment or something." Reminding himself of his forced abstinence, he took his large cigar case from an inner pocket.

"Is Nils here now?" Arnie asked.

"He took off right away," Ove told him. "They're using the ship for a television relay and he is holding position above the horizon."

"Back of the Moon, that's the way," Leif Holm said, clipping off the end of his immense cigar with a cutter hung from his watch chain. "So they can't watch us with their damned great telescopes."

"I haven't had a chance to congratulate you yet," Ove said.

"Very kind, thank you. Minister for Space. It has a good sound to it. I also don't have to worry what my predecessors did—since I don't have any."

"If you will please take your places we can have the briefing now," the State Ministry man said, hurrying in. He was beginning to sweat. Arnie and Leif Holm sat behind the table, and someone went running for an ashtray. "Here are the main points we want to mention." He laid the stapled sheets in front of both of them. "I know you have been briefed, but these will be of help in any case. Minister Holm, you will make your opening statements. Then the journalists on Earth will ask questions. The technical ones will be answered by Professor Klein."

"Who are the journalists?" Arnie asked. "From what countries?"

"Top people. A tough crowd. The Soviets and Americans, of course, and the major European countries. The other countries have been pooled and have elected their own representatives. There are about twenty-five in all."

"Israeli?"

"Yes. They insisted on having a representative of their own. All things considered, you know, we agreed."

"The link is open," the director called out "Stand by. Three minutes. We are tied into Eurovision, by satellite to the Americas and Asia. Top viewing. Just watch the monitor and you will know when you are on."

A television set with a large screen was placed under camera one. The picture was adequate, the scene tense. The Danish announcer was finishing the introduction, in English, the language that would be used for this broadcast.

". . . from all over the world, gathered here in Copenhagen today, to talk to them on the Moon. It must be remembered that it takes radio waves nearly two seconds to reach the Moon, and the same amount of time to return, so there will be this amount of time between question and reply during the latter half of this session. We will now switch you over to the Danish Moon Station, to Mr. Leif Holm, the Minister for Space."

The red light glowed on camera two, and they appeared on the monitor screen. Leif Holm carefully tapped his ash into the ashtray and inhaled from his cigar, so that his first words were accompanied by a generous cloud of smoke.

"I am speaking from the Moon, where Denmark has established a base for research and commercial development of the Daleth drive that has permitted these flights. The construction is in its earliest stages—you can see the operation continuing behind me through the window—and will continue until there is a small city here. For the beginning this base will be dedicated to scientific research, to continue the development of the Daleth drive that has made this all possible. In one sense this portion of the work is already completed because all"—he leaned forward to stare grimly at the camera—"*all* of the Daleth project is now at this base. Professor Klein, sitting on my right, is here to direct the research. He has brought his assistants with him, all of his equipment, records, everything to do with this project." He leaned back and drew on his cigar again before continuing.

"You will excuse my insistence on this fact, but I wish to make it clear. Denmark in the past months has suffered many acts of violence within her borders. Crimes have been committed. People have been killed. It is sad to admit but there are national powers on Earth that will go to any lengths to obtain information about the Daleth drive. I speak to them now, and I beg forgiveness in advance from all of the peace-loving countries of the world, the overwhelming majority. You can stop now. Leave. There is nothing for you to steal. We in Denmark intend to develop the Daleth effect for the greater benefit of mankind. Not for violence."

He stopped, almost glaring at the screen, then leaned back. Arnie was staring straight ahead, expressionless, as he had done during the entire talk.

"We will now answer any specific questions that you may have."

The scene on the monitor changed to the auditorium in Copenhagen where the press representatives waited. They sat on chairs, in neat rows, in attitudes of silent attention, while slow seconds slipped by. It was disconcerting to realize that radio waves, even at the speed of light, took measurable seconds to cross the great distance between the Moon and Earth. In an abrupt, galvanic change the scene altered as a number of the newsmen jumped to their feet, clamoring for attention. One of them was recognized and the cameras focused on him, a burly man with a great shock of hair. The white letters UNITED STATES OF AMERICA appeared below him on the screen.

"Can you tell us who is making these alleged attacks in Denmark? These so called 'national powers,' to use your own term, in the plural, could, by inference, mean any country. Therefore all the countries stand condemned by innuendo. This is highly unfair." He glowered at the camera.

"I am sorry that you find it so," Holm responded calmly. "But it's the truth. Attacks have occurred. People have died. It is unimportant to go into the question further. Surely the world press must have more relevant questions than this one."

Before the angry reporter could answer, another man was recognized, the representative of the Soviet Union who, if he was also angry, managed to conceal it very well.

"Of course the Union of Soviet Socialist Republics joins in with all the peace-loving nations of the world to condemn the acts of aggression that have occurred in Denmark." He exchanged a look of mutual hatred with the American reporter, then went on. "A more important question would be, What does your country intend to do with this Daleth drive?"

"We intend to exploit it commercially," Holm answered after the mandatory seconds had passed. "In the same way that Danish shipping opened up the commerical possibilities of East Asia during the last century. A company has been formed, *Det Forenede Rumskibsselskab*, The United Spaceship Company, a partnership between the government and private industry. We mean to open up the Moon and the planets. At this time there are of course no specific plans, but we are sure that great opportunities lie ahead. Raw materials, research, tourism—who knows where it will end? We in Denmark are most enthusiastic, because at this time we see no end to the good that will come from it."

"Good for Denmark," the Russian said before another questioner could be recognized. "Does not this monopoly mean that you will deprive the rest of the world of fair share in the venture? Should you not, as a socialist country, share your discovery in the true socialist spirit?"

Leif Holm nodded solemn agreement. "Though many of our public institutions are socialistic, enough of our private ones are sufficiently capitalistic to keep us from giving away what you have called a 'monopoly.' It is a monopoly only in the sense that we shall operate the Daleth ships, at a fair profit, that will open up the solar system to all the countries of the Earth. We will try not to be greedy. We have already entered into an agreement with other Scandinavian countries for the manufacture of the ships. Our belief is that this invention will benefit all of mankind, and we consider it our duty to implement that belief."

The representative of the Israeli press was recognized from the crowd of excited, waving men, and he addressed the camera. He had a detached, scholarly manner, with a tendency to look over the top of his rimless glasses, but Arnie recognized him as one of the shrewdest commentators that country had.

"If this discovery is of such a great benefit to mankind, I would like to ask why it has not been made available to the entire world? My question is directed to Professor Klein."

Arnie had short seconds to prepare his answer—but he had been expecting the question. He looked directly into the camera and spoke slowly and clearly.

"The Daleth effect is more than a means of propulsion. It could be turned to destructive uses with ease. A country with the will to conquer the world *could* conquer the world through utilization of this effect. Or destroy the world in the attempt."

"Could you elaborate? I am anxious to discover how this species of rocket ship engine could do all you say."

He smiled, but Arnie knew better than to believe the smile. They both knew more about the history of the Daleth effect than they were admitting aloud.

"It can do more because it is *not* a kind of rocket engine. It is a new principle. It can be applied to lift a small ship—or a large ship. Or even an entire concrete-and-steel fortress mounting the heaviest cannon, and to take this anywhere in the world in a matter of minutes. It could hang in space, on top of the gravity well, immune from any retaliation by rockets, even atom-bomb-equipped rockets, and could destroy any target it wished with bombs or shells. Or if that image is not horrific enough for you, the Daleth effect could be made to pick up great boulders—or even small mountains—from here on the Moon, and drop them on Earth. There is no limit to the imaginable destruction."

"And you feel that the other countries of the world would use the Daleth effect for destruction if they had it?" The other reporters were silent for the moment, recognizing the underplay in the dialogue between the two men.

"You know they would," Arnie snapped back. "Since when has the horrible potential of a weapon stopped it from being used? The cultures who have practiced genocide, used poison gas and atom bombs in warfare, will stop at nothing."

"And you felt that Israel would do these things? Since I understand you first developed the Daleth effect in Israel and took it from this country."

Arnie had been expecting this, but he still wilted visibly beneath the blow. When he spoke again his voice was so low that the engineers had to turn up the volume of their transmission.

"I did not wish to see Israel forced to choose between her survival and the unleashing of great evil upon the world. At first I considered destroying my papers, until I realized that there was a very good chance that someone else might reach the same conclusions and make the same discovery that I did.

I was forced to come to a decision—and I did." He was angry now, defiant in his words.

"To the best of my knowledge I did the right thing, and I would do it over again if I were forced to. I brought my discovery to Denmark because, as much as I love Israel, it is a country at war, that might eventually be forced to use the Daleth effect for war. It was my belief that if I found a way for my work to benefit all mankind, Israel would benefit too. Benefit first, for all that I owe her. But Denmark—I know this country, I was born there—could never be tempted into war by aggression. This is the country that twice almost voted unilateral disarmament for itself. In a world of tigers they wished to go unarmed! They have faith. I have faith in them. I could be wrong but, God save me, I have done the best I could. . . ."

His voice choked with emotion, and he looked away from the camera. The director instantly switched the scene back to Earth. After the moments of waiting an Indian reporter was recognized, the representative of an Asiatic reporter pool.

"Would the Minister of Space be so kind as to elaborate upon the benefits to accrue from the utilization of this discovery and to suggest, if possible, what specific benefits there might be for the countries of southern Asia?"

"I can do that," Holm said, and looked down at his cigar, surprised to see that he had completely forgotten it, and that it had gone out.

18

RUNGSTED KYST

"It's a perfect day for it," Martha Hansen said, rubbing out the cigarette in the ashtray, then clasping her hands together to conceal how excited she was.

"It certainly is, it certainly is," Skou said, his nose pushed forward, looking around as though sniffing out trouble. "Will you excuse me for a moment?"

He was gone before Martha could answer, with his two shadows trailing after him. She shook another cigarette out of the pack and lighted it; at this rate she would have a pack smoked before noon. She twisted about, with her legs up on the couch, smoothing down her skirt. Had she worn the right thing? The knitted dress was always Nils's favorite. How long had it been? She turned quickly when she heard a car—but it was only the traffic passing on Strandvejen. The sun burned down on a scene of green grass, tall trees, and the bright blue waters of the Sound beyond. White sails leaned away from the wind and a bee-buzzing motorboat drew a pale line of wake toward Sweden. A June Sunday with the sun shining—Denmark could be heaven, and Nils was coming home! How many months . . .

It was practically a convoy, three large black cars, pulling into the drive and stopping before the house. A police car and another car parked at the curb beyond them. They were here. She ran, getting there ahead of Skou, throwing the door wide.

"Martha!" he shouted, dropping his bag and sweeping her to him, kissing her so hard she had no breath, right there on the porch. She managed to push free, laughing, when she realized that a small circle of men was waiting patiently for them to finish.

"I'm sorry, please come in," she said, aware that her hair was mussed and her lipstick probably smeared, and not giving a damn. "Arnie, it is wonderful to see you. Come in please." Then they were in the living room, just the three of them, with the sound of heavy feet stamping through the rest of the house.

"I'm sorry about the honor guard," Nils said. "But it was the only way we could get Arnie back to Earth for a holiday. It was time for us all to have a break, and I think maybe him most of all. Watchdog Skou agreed on it as long as Arnie stayed with us, and Skou could make all the security arrangements he wanted to."

"Thank you for having me," Arnie said, leaning back wearily in the upholstered chair. He looked drawn and had lost a lot of weight. "I am sorry to impose . . ."

"Don't be silly! If you say another word I shall throw you out and make you stay at the Mission Hotel which, as you know, is absolutely non-alcoholic. Here you get drinks. To celebrate. What would you like?" She stood and opened the bar.

"My arms feel heavy as lead," Nils said, scowling as he moved his hand up and down. "I've barely enough strength to lift a glass to my mouth. That gravity, one-sixth of Earth's, it ruins the muscles."

"Poor dear! Shall I bottle feed you?"

"You know what you can do to give me strength!"

"You sound too exhausted. Better have a drink first. I've made a pitcher of martinis—all right?"

"Fine. And remind me, I have a bottle of Bombay gin in my suitcase for you. We have it tax-free on the Moon, since they have decided to call it a free-port area until someone comes up with a better idea. The customs men, very generous, allow us to bring one bottle back. An 800,000 kilometer round trip to save twenty-five kroner in duty. The world's mad." He took a deep drag on the chilled drink and sighed with pleasure.

Arnie sipped at his. "I hope you will excuse all the guards and fuss, but they treat me like a national treasure—"

"As you damn well are!" Nils broke in. "With all the Daleth equipment on the Moon, you are worth a billion kroner on the hoof to any country with the money to buy you. I wish I weren't so patriotic. I would sell you to the highest bidder and retire to Bali for life."

Arnie smiled, almost relaxing.

"They had a conspiracy. The doctors, Skou, your husband, all of them. They thought if they made an armed fort of your home that I could come here. The weather could not be better."

"Sailing weather," Nils said, and drained his drink. "Where's the boat?"

"In the water, like you asked, tied up on the south side of the harbor."

"What a day for sailing! Why don't we all go down there—no, damn, Arnie's supposed to stay in the house."

"You two go, I will be fine right here," Arnie insisted. "I will get some sun in the garden, that is what Nils promised me."

"No such thing," Martha said. "Nils is going to the harbor and get all hot and tarry. He never sails the boat, just caulks seams and things. Let him get it out of his system while we loaf in the garden."

"Well—if you don't mind?" Nils was already leaning toward the door.

"Go on," Martha laughed. "Just come back in time for dinner."

"I'll find Skou and tell him where I'm going. Not that they care about me, since all I know about a Daleth drive is how to push the buttons."

Martha had to find him his work trousers, then a paint-stained shirt, then his swim trunks before he was ready and slammed out of the house. Arnie had gone to his room to change and, at the sight of all the delicious sunlight, Martha put on a bathing suit too. All Danes were sun worshipers on a day like this.

Arnie was on a lounge on the patio, and she pulled the other one up next to him.

"Wonderful," he said. "I did not realize how much we miss color and being out of doors." The shadow of a gull slid across the grass and up the high wooden fence. The air was still. Someone laughed, far away, and there was the distinct plock-plock of a tennis ball being played.

"How is the work going? Or as much of it as you can tell me about."

"The only secret is the drive. For the rest it is like running a steamship company and opening up the wild West at the same time. Did you read about our Mars visit?"

"Yes, I was so jealous. When do you start selling passenger tickets?"

"Very soon. And you will have the very first one. There really are plans being made along those lines. In any case, those surface veins of uranium on Mars made the DFRS stock soar tremendously on the world markets. Money is being poured into the super-liner that the Swedes are building, mostly for cargo, but with plenty of cabins for passengers later. We will lift her by tug to the Moon and put the drive in there. The base is almost a city now, with machine shops and assembly plants. We do almost all of the manufacturing of the Daleth units there, except for standard electronics components from here. It is all going so well, no one can complain." He looked around for a piece of wood to touch, and found none among the chrome-and-plastic garden furniture.

"Shall I bring you a board or something?" Martha asked, and they both laughed. "Or better yet bring you a cold drink. The yard, closed in like this, cuts off the breeze, and you can actually work up a sweat in this kind of weather."

"Yes, please, if you will join me."

"Try and stop me. Gin and tonic since we already started on gin."

She came back with the drinks on a tray, silently on her bare feet, and Arnie started when he saw her.

"I didn't mean to surprise you," she said, handing him a glass.

"Please do not blame yourself. I know that it is I. There has been a great deal of work and tension. So it is really very good to be here. In fact it is almost as hot as Israel."

"Do you miss Israel?" she asked, then quickly said, "I'm sorry. I know that it's none of my business."

The smile was gone, his face set. "Yes, I miss the country. My friends, the life there. But I think that I would do the entire thing over again in the same manner if I were given a second chance."

"I don't mean to pry. . . ."

"No, Martha, it is perfectly all right. It is on my mind a good deal of the time. Traitor or hero? I myself would rather die than cause injury to Israel. Yet I had a letter, in Hebrew, no signature. 'What would Esther Bar-Giora have thought?' it said."

"Your wife?"

"Yes. She looked very much like you. The same kind of hair and"—he glanced at her figure, more flesh than fabric in the diminutive bathing suit, and looked away and coughed—"the, what you might call, the same sort of build. But dark, tanned all the time. A sabra, born and grew up in Israel. One of my graduate students. She married the professor, she used to always say." His eyes had a distant, haunted look. "She was killed in a terror raid." He sipped his drink. In the silence that followed the distant shouting of children could be heard.

"But do not let me sound too gloomy, Martha. It is too nice an afternoon. I would like to have known who sent that letter. I wanted to tell whoever it was that I think Esther would have been angry at me, but she would have understood. And in the end she might even have agreed with me. There must be a time when the issue of all mankind should come ahead of our concerns with our own country. You should know about that, what I mean. Born an American, now a Dane, a real citizen of the world."

"No, not really." She laughed to cover her confusion. "I mean I am married to a Dane, but I am still an American citizen, passport and all." Now why had she told him about that?

"Papers," he said, lifting his hand in a gesture of dismissal. "Meaningless. We are what we think we are. Our deeds reflect our ethos. I am stating it badly. I never did well in philosophy, or in anything other than physics and mathematics. I even failed stinks once, forgot a retort on the burner and let it explode. And I never thought much about anything other than my work. And Esther, of course, when we were married. People used to call me a dry stick, and they were right. I never played cards, nothing like that. But I could see and I could think. And watch the attempts to destroy Israel. And when the idea of the Daleth drive came closer and closer to reality, I thought more and more about what should be done with it. I remembered Nobel and his million-dollar guilty-conscience awards. I thought of the atomic scientists who had been certified or who had committed suicide. Why, I kept thinking, why can't something be done *before* the discovery is revealed? Can I not turn it to the benefit of mankind instead of the destruction? The thought stayed with me, and I could not get rid of it, and—in the end—I had to act upon it. I did not think that it would be easy, but I never thought it would be this hard . . ."

Arnie broke off and sipped at his drink. "You must excuse me; I am talking too much. The company of men. A woman, a sympathetic ear, and you see what happens. A joke." He smiled a twisted grin.

"No, never!" She leaned over impulsively and took his hand. "A woman would go mad if she couldn't tell her troubles to someone. I think that's the trouble with men. They hold it all in until they explode and then go out and kill someone."

"Yes, of course. Thank you. Thank you very much." He patted her hand clumsily with his and lay back heavily, eyes closed. A fat bumblebee hummed industriously around the hollyhock that climbed the side of the house, the only sound now in the still of the afternoon.

* * *

"Den er fin med kompasset,
Sla rommen i glasset . . ."

Nils sang happily in a loud monotone, scraping away at the paint blister on the cockpit cover. The harbor was deserted; on a summer Sunday like this every boat was out in the Sound. He would be too, as soon as he finished this job. He hated to see any imperfections on his *Mage*, so he ended up doing much more painting and polishing than sailing. Well, that was fun too. He had muscles and he liked to use them. Though they would ache tomorrow after the months of enervating lunar gravity. He was barefoot, stripped to his swim trunks, sweating greatly and enjoying himself tremendously. Singing so loud that he was unaware of the quiet footsteps on the dock behind him.

"That's a terrible noise that you are making," the voice said.

"Inger!" He sat up and wiped his hands on the rag. "Do you make a habit of sneaking up on me? And what the devil are you doing here?"

"Accident, if you can call fate that. I'm with friends from the Malmö Yacht Club, we're just out for the day." She pointed at a large cabin cruiser on the other side of the harbor. "We tied up here for lunch—and some drinks of course, you know how thirsty we Swedes get. They all went into the kro. I have to join them."

"Not before I give you a drink—I have some bottles of beer in a bucket. My God but you look good."

She did indeed. Inger Ahlqvist. Six feet of honey-tanned blonde, in a bikini so small that it was hardly noticeable.

"You shouldn't walk around like that in public," he said, aware of the tightening of the muscles in his stomach, his thighs. "It's just criminal. And torture to a poor guy who has been playing Man in the Moon for so long that he has forgotten what a girl even looks like."

"They look like me," she said, and laughed. "Come on, give me that beer so I can go get my lunch. Sailing is hungry work. How is the Moon?"

"Indescribable. But you'll be there one of these days soon. DFRS will need hostesses, and we'll bribe you away from SAS." He jumped down into the cockpit, landing heavier than he realized, still not adjusted to the change in gravity, and opened the cabin door. "I'll get one for myself too. Isn't this the weather? What have you been doing?"

He went to the far end where he had the green bottles in a bucket of water with chunks of ice. She stepped into the cockpit and leaned down to talk to him.

"The same old round. Still fun, but don't think I haven't envied you all this Moon and Mars travel. Do you mean what you said about the hostess thing?"

"Of course." He clicked the caps off both bottles with an opener fixed to the bulkhead. "No details yet, secret and all that, but there are definite plans for passenger runs in the future. There have to be. Do you realize that we can reach the Moon base faster than the regular flight can go from Kastrup to New York? Here."

He handed her the bottle and she stepped forward to get it.

"Skal."

She drank deeply, lowered the bottle with a contented sigh, her lips full and damp. Just inches away. There was no thought involved.

His bottle dropped to the deck, rolled, spilling out a pale stream of foam. His arms were around her back, the flesh of his hands against the warmth of her skin, her thighs tight to his thighs, the pressure of her breasts flattening against him. Her mouth was open, her lips beer-moist against his.

Her bottle dropped, rolled, clattered against the others.

They did not hear it. They were falling.

* * *

Arnie's mouth was slightly open, and his head had fallen over to one side; he was breathing deeply and regularly. Martha rose slowly so as not to disturb him. If she stayed in the still heat of the garden any longer she would fall asleep too, and she did not want to do that. She went into the house and slipped into a light beach jacket, then knocked on Skou's door. He opened it, wearing a pair of earphones, and waved her in. He had converted the back bedroom into a command post and there was a table full of communications equipment. He issued instructions and switched off.

"I'm going to the harbor for a bit," she told him. "Professor Klein is asleep in the back yard and I didn't want to bother him."

"That's our job, watching him. I'll tell him where you went if he wakes up."

It was only a five-minute walk. Martha went along the beach, carrying her sandals. The sand was warm and felt good between her toes. She stayed away from the water, which she knew, even now, would be far too cold for swimming. The air was still, almost soundless except for the flut-flutting of a helicopter overhead. Probably part of the guard for Arnie. There were a number of extra cars and trucks parked in her neighborhood, and she knew that some of the neighbors had unexpected guests. That poor, tired little man was being guarded like a national treasure. Well he probably was one. She waved to a party of friends sunning themselves on the beach, and climbed the stone steps to the top of the seawall. The harbor was almost empty of boats, and there was *Mage*—but Nils was nowhere to be seen.

Perhaps he had gone across the road to the kro for a drink? No, he usually stopped there on the way to get some bottles of beer. Where could he have gotten to? Below decks probably.

She was about to call to him when she saw the beer bottle on the cockpit floor, and next to it, trailing through the half-open door, a piece of blue fabric. The halter top of a bikini.

In that single instant, with heart-stopping clarity, she knew what she would see if she looked into the cabin. As though she had lived this instant before, sometime, and had buried the memory which was not surfacing. Calmly—why? she wasn't feeling calm—she stepped forward to the edge of the dock and leaned far out, holding onto the bollard anchored there. Through the door she could now see the starboard bunk, Nils's broad back, and what he was doing. The arms that were tightly pressed against that back, the tanned legs . . . .

With a muffled sob she straightened up, feeling a hot wave of anger sweeping over her, reddening her skin. Here, in their boat, after being away all this time, not even home yet!

Ready to jump into the boat, ready to hurt, bite, tear, she did not want to hold back. But there was shouting, loud noise. She looked up.

"The sail is stuck!" someone shouted in Danish from the single-masted yacht that was rushing in toward the dock, almost on top of her.

There was a brief glimpse of a man wrestling with the fouled rigging, a woman pushing at the tiller, screeching something at him, and children grabbing for ropes and falling over each other. At any other time it would have been funny. They were coming on, still too fast, and the woman jammed the tiller hard over.

Instead of striking bow on, the boat turned, hitting a glancing blow to the pilings, bouncing away. One of the small children fell off the cabin roof onto the deck and began to shriek in fright. The sail came down in a jumble and the man fought with it.

Then they lost way and bobbed to a stop. Tragedy averted. Someone even began to laugh. It had only taken seconds. Martha started forward again—then hesitated. In those brief instants everything had changed. They would be sitting up, pulling on clothing, laughing perhaps. She felt embarrassment at the thought, and hesitated. She was still as angry, though the anger was choked within her. The little yacht was tying up a few feet away. Could she, coldly now, enter that cabin, scream at them with these others here? A boy brushed against her, apologizing as he fastened one of the lines.

With a gasp, something between pain and hatred, she turned, fled, running, slowing down. Anger, terrible anger burning her. How could he have done this! She gasped again.

Only when she reached the front door of her home did she realize that she was still carrying her sandals and that the soles of her feet were sore from the concrete sidewalk. Shaking, she put them on and remembered that she had no key. She raised her fist, but before she could knock Skou opened the door for her.

"Watchfulness is our password," he said, letting her in and then closing and locking the door behind her.

She nodded, went by him, unseeing. Watchfulness . . . that was very funny, it should be her password too. She didn't want to talk to him, to see anyone. She went past quickly and on into the bathroom. Anger was burning her now, tightening her throat, impotent anger that she could do nothing about. She shouldn't have run away! But what else could she have done? With a sob of rage she turned the cold water full on, plunged her arms into it, splashed water onto her burning face. She could not even cry, her rage was too strong. How could he! How could he!

She ran her fingers through her hair, unable to face herself in the mirror. If he was not ashamed, she was. She stroked at her hair violently with the brush. Married men did things like this, she knew that—a lot of them in Denmark. But not Nils. Why not Nils? Now she knew. Had he done it before? What could she do now? What could she do about him?

With this thought she had a sudden image of him coming home, here, wanting to embrace her just as if nothing had happened. He would do that—and what would *she* do? Could she tell him? Did she want him? Yes. *No*! She wanted to hurt him just the way he had hurt her. What he had done was unforgivable.

Her throat was tight and she had the sensation that she would break into tears at any moment, and she did not want to. What was there to cry about? What the *hell* was there to cry about? There was plenty enough to be angry about.

She stood quickly, wanting to get away from her reflected image. As she did she saw the little spiral-bound notebook on top of the laundry container, and she picked it up because it did not belong there. When she opened it automatically, wondering what to do with it, she saw that the pages were covered with rows of neat calculations, more strangely shaped symbols than numbers. She closed it quickly and went to her room, shutting the door and pressing her back to it, the notebook held tight against her breasts.

If emotion can be said to replace the logical order of rational thinking, this was surely one of the times. Baxter had scarcely bothered her of late, but she was not really thinking about Baxter. Or about America and Denmark, or loyalty or patriotism. She was thinking about Nils and what she had seen and, perhaps, though she was not aware of it, she wanted to hurt him in the way he had hurt her.

It was all quite easy to do. Locking the door behind her, Martha went to her bureau and took the camera out of the drawer. She had put film in it just yesterday, getting ready for Nils's homecoming, fast color film to make a permanent record of this holiday. There was a patch of sunlight on the rug by the bed, streaming in the open window. She put the notebook on the floor and opened it to the first page. When she sat on the edge of the bed above it and looked through the viewfinder it was just right. Just one meter, the closest she could take a picture without blurring it. The image of the pages was sharp and clear and the camera automatically set the exposure.

click

She advanced the film, bent over to turn the page, then braced her elbows on her knees again.

There were still ten frames left when she finished the last page. So she took pictures of the back and front covers because she hated to waste film. Then she realized that this was just being foolish, so she closed the camera case and put it back into the drawer. She took the notebook and unlocked the door and went out, and met Arnie coming up the stairs.

"Martha," he said, blinking in the darkness after the glare outside. "I woke up suddenly and realized that I had misplaced my notebook."

She shrank back slightly, her hand—and the notebook—pressed tightly to her.

"There it is!" he said, and pointed. He smiled. "How nice of you to find it for me."

"I was taking it to your room," she said in a voice that

sounded shrill and artificial, but he did not seem to notice. She held it out.

"And right you were too. If Skou found it lying around he would probably have me returned to the Moon at once. Thank you. I shall just lock it in my case so I will not be this foolish again. I am sorry I fell asleep like that. Some guest! But I feel much better for it. It has been a wonderful day."

She nodded slow agreement as he went into his room.

19

The Jaguar saloon moved steadily north along the coast, staying exactly at the posted speed limit. Nils drove easily with one hand while he tried to find some music on the radio.

"We are starting out a little late," he said. "Do you have to stop in Helsingor?"

"I have to go to the post office. It will only take a minute," Martha said.

"What's so important?" He found a Swedish station that was playing a peasant polka, all yipping and stomping.

"I have to send off some film for developing."

"What's wrong with the photography shop next to the grocer in Rungsted?"

"They're too slow. This is a special place in Copenhagen. If you think I'll make you late just drop me off by the ferry and you can go on by yourself."

He took a quick look out of the corner of his eye, but she was looking ahead, her face expressionless.

"Come on! This is a holiday—of course I'll wait. I just don't want us to miss the launching—or ascension or whatever you want to call it. You'll love it. These tugs will just drift down and latch onto the ship and lift it right up out of the ways. They'll install the drive on the Moon."

They had to wait at the ferry ship while a fussy little steam engine pulled a string of Swedish boxcars across the road.

"Look at that yard donkey," Nils said. "Leaking steam and oil from every joint—and still dragging trains off the ferry. Do you know how old it is?" Martha apparently did not know, nor did she appear too interested in the answer. "I'll tell you. It's on that plate on the side of the cab. Eighteen ninety-two that antique was built, and still on the job. We Danes never throw anything away while it still works. A very practical people."

"As opposed to we Americans who build cars and things to break down at once and be discarded?"

He did not answer, but drove past the station and turned down Jernbanevej to the post office at the rear of the terminal. He parked and she got out, carrying the small package. Film. He wondered how long she had had it in the camera. She certainly had not taken any pictures since this holiday began. Some holiday. Bitchy, he thought, during my entire leave. He wondered what could possibly be bothering her; he could think of nothing. He saw that he had parked next to a hot dog stand, and his stomach gave an interested rumble at the sight. They would be sure to have a late lunch and he ought to be prepared. He went in and ordered two of them—raw onion, ketchup and mustard—then canceled the onion when he remembered that they would be at the launching with all the politicians and bigwigs. He had to remember this place; they had beer too, so he washed the *polser* down with a cold bottle of Tuborg Gold.

What was the matter with Martha? She was not unresponsive, but there was a coldness that made her roll away from him in bed at night. Perhaps it was the tension of the Moon flights, the sabotage and all that. You never could tell about women. Funny damn creatures. Given to moods. He saw her coming out of the post office and hurriedly finished the beer.

Nils never had a moment of doubt. Nor had he once, ever since that Sunday afternoon, ever even thought about Inger.

20

MARS

It was almost noon, so that here on the equator, at midsummer, the temperature had shot up to almost 30 degrees below freezing. The hill, really one flank of a great circular crater, rose up sharply from the plain. A much shrunken sun glared down on the frozen landscape from a black sky, where the brightest stars could be easily seen. Only at the horizon was the atmosphere dense enough to trace a thin line of blue against the sky. The air was still, with a timeless silence, so thin, almost pure carbon dioxide, that it was almost not air at all. And very, very cold.

The two men climbing the steep slope had hard going despite the lower gravity. Their heavily insulated, electrically heated clothing hampered their movements; their battery packs and oxygen tanks weighed them down. When they reached the crest they stopped, gratefully, to rest. Their features were hidden by their masks and goggles.

"That's . . . quite a climb," Arnie said, gasping for breath.

No expression could be seen on Nils's shrouded face, but his voice was worried. "I hope it wasn't too much. Maybe I shouldn't have brought you?"

"Fine. Just out of breath. And out of shape. It has been too long since I have done anything like this. But it is worth it, really, a simply magnificent sight."

The silent landscape reduced them, too, to silence. Chill, dark, alien, a planet that had not died because it had never been born. The tiny settlement below was like a welcoming light in a window, a single touch of warmth in the eternal cold of Mars. Arnie looked around—then stepped quickly aside, beckoning Nils after him.

"Is anything wrong?" Nils asked.

"No, not at all. We were just standing between the sun and this *Mars-kal*. It is starting to close up. It thinks that it is night again."

The foot-long and widespread starfish-like arms of the animal-plant were half closed, revealing the rough, grayish underside. When completely closed they formed a ball, insulated against this incredibly harsh environment, holding tight to the minuscule amount of heat and energy the animal-plant had obtained, waiting for the sun to return once again. When it did, the arms would unfold to reveal the shiny black plates of their undersides, which captured and stored the radiation from the far distant sun. This tough growth was the only form of life discovered yet on Mars and, although its nickname "Mars cabbage" was now the official title, it was looked upon with respect, if not with awe, by all of them. This was the only Martian. Both men stood carefully aside so that the sunlight could fall on it again.

"It reminds me of some of the desert plants in Israel," Arnie said.

"Do you miss Israel?" Nils asked.

"Yes, of course. You do not have to ask." Because of the thin atmosphere his voice was a distant whisper, despite the fact he was talking loudly.

"I imagine you would. I know a lot of countries, and most of them look a lot more interesting than Denmark when first you fly in. I could live in any of them, I suppose, but I would still pick Denmark. I wouldn't like to leave. I sometimes wonder how you managed to pack up and leave Israel on principle. I doubt if I could do a thing like that. Doubt if I would have the guts to do it myself." He pointed. "Look, there it is, just like I told you. You can see the entire area from up here. There are the new buildings, just going up, and the landing area laid out beyond *Galathea*. When they will be needed, more buildings can be constructed along the eastern side. There is going to be an entire settlement here—a city some day. The railroad will go from right down there to the mountains where the mines will be."

"A very optimistic project. But there is certainly no reason why it should not work out that way." But Arnie was thinking about what Nils had said. About Israel. It was a topic that he worried to himself, like a sore tooth, and he could not stay away from it. Although he rarely talked about it to anyone else. "What did you mean, exactly, when you said that what I did took guts? I did only what I had to do. Do you think that it was wrong—that I owed Israel loyalty ahead of all mankind!"

"Hell, no!" the big pilot said, and managed to get a boom of warmth into the whisper of his audible voice. "I'm on your side, don't ever forget that. What I really mean is that I admire what you did, not selling out. If what you say is true, then staying would have been the big sellout. The same way that scientists have been selling out since the word science was invented. Bombs, poison gas, and death for the sake of my fatherland. That's the direct sellout. Invent the atom bomb—then moan about the way it is being used but don't stick your neck out. The indirect sellout. Or the wool-over-the-eyes sellout: I'm working on nerve gases, germ warfare, bigger bombs, but they will never be used. Or the world-is-too-big-for-me-to-do-anything sellout, the one everyone uses. Dow Chemical makes napalm to cook people. But I can't stop buying Dow products, it won't make any difference. South Africa has the best police state in the world and a country full of legal Negro slaves. But I'll still buy their oranges, what can I do? You can blame yourself for how I feel, Arnie."

"What on Earth—I mean what on Mars—do you mean?" He stamped his feet as the cold began to seep through the soles of his boots.

"I mean that you did what I think I would not have had the guts to do. You stuck by your convictions, no matter what your personal loss. There have been all kinds of Dow and South Africa boycotts in Denmark, and I ignored them. Or laughed at them. What could *I* do? I flew and I lived well and I enjoyed myself. But you got under my skin, showed me something different . . ."

"Stop!" Arnie said, shocked. "You don't realize what you are saying, I did a traitorous thing, betraying my country and her trust in me and depriving her of the results of the research that rightly belonged there. I went outside the law. If a scientist can be said to have an oath, I have surely violated mine."

"I don't understand—"

"I am sure you don't. Your view is one-sided, unthinking, even more biased than mine. I admit my crime. Yet you offhandedly blame all scientists for all the sins of the world. You speak of atomic bombs. But what of atomic power plants and radioactive medicines? You blame scientists for inventing explosives, but don't talk about the plastics that stem from the same chemical fundamentals. You speak of bacterial warfare, but not about the virus-killing medicines that came from the same research. You may try, but you cannot blame science and scientists for the world's ills. We physicists may have made the atom bomb, but it was the government that financed it and elected politicians who decided to drop it. And the people at large seemed to have approved of the decision. Scientists don't make war—it is *people* who do. If you try and blame the scientists for the condition of the world, you are just using them as scapegoats. It is far easier to blame another person than to admit one's own guilt. Enough South Africans must enjoy being legal slave owners or their government would not stay in power. Remember what the face of the active opposition of the people. The Nazis did not exterminate the Jews—the German people did. People have the responsibility of their deeds, but they do not like the weight of this responsibility. They therefore choose to blame others. They say that the scientists, who invented bombs and planes and guns, are responsible for the state of the world today. But the people who elect the politicians who make the wars are blameless. Do you really think that it is that way?"

Nils was shocked at the sudden anger. "I didn't mean it like that. I just said I admired—"

"Don't admire a man who has betrayed his country's trust

in him. Even if my decision proves correct, I have still done an unforgivable thing."

"If you feel this way, why did you leave Israel at all and come to Denmark? I know that you were born in Denmark and grew up there. Was that the reason why?"

The Martian silence closed in for long seconds before Arnie spoke again.

"Perhaps. Or perhaps because of faith—or hope. Or maybe because I am a Jew. In Israel I was an Israeli. But everywhere else in the world I am a Jew. Except in Denmark. There are no Jews in Denmark—just a lot of Danes of varying religious faiths. You were just three or four years old when the Nazis marched across Europe, so it is only history to you, another chapter in the thick books. They are monsters—demons in that they could unlock the evil in other hearts as well as their own. The people in the countries they conquered ***helped*** them fuel the ovens. The French police went out and arrested Jews for them. The Ukrainians happily fed the furnaces for them. The Poles rushed to see their Jewish neighbors cooked, only to be melted down themselves for their loyalty. Every invaded country helped the Germans. Every country except one. In Denmark the police were shocked to hear of the coming purge. They passed the word to others who were equally horrified. Cab drivers cruised the streets with telephone books, looking for people with Jewish names. Boy Scouts passed the warnings. Every hospital in the land opened its doors to the Jews and hid them. In a few days every Jew who could be reached was smuggled safely out of the country. Do you know why the Danes did this?"

"Of course!" He clenched his large fists. "Those were human beings, Danes. That sort of thing just isn't done."

"So—you have answered your own question. I had a choice and I made it. I pray that I was right."

Arnie started down the hill, then stopped for a moment.

"I was one of the people smuggled out to Sweden. So perhaps I am repaying a debt."

They went down, side by side, to the light and warmth of the base.

21

COPENHAGEN

"There's no point in our taking both cars," Martha said into the telephone. "We can fight about which one later, all right. . . . Yes, Ove. . . . Is Ulla ready? . . . Good. I'll be there in about an hour, I guess. . . . Yes, that should give us plenty of time. We have those seats in the reserved section and everything, so there shouldn't be any trouble. Listen, my doorbell just rang. Everything's all set? . . . See you then."

She hung up hurriedly and went to get her housecoat as the bell rang again. All she had to do was finish her face and put her dress on—but she wasn't going to answer the door in her slip.

"Ja, nu kommer jeg," she called out, hurrying down the hall. When she opened the door she stopped halfway, as soon as she saw the pendant bundle of brushes; a door-to-door peddler.

"Nej tak, ingen pensler idag."

"You had better let me in," the man said. "I have to talk to you."

The sudden English startled her and she looked past the well-worn suit and cap, at the man's face. His watery blue eyes, blinking, red-rimmed.

"Mr. Baxter! I didn't recognize you at first. . . ." Without the dark-rimmed glasses he seemed a totally different man.

"I can't stand at the door like this," he said angrily. "Let me in."

He pushed toward her and she stepped aside to let him by, then closed the door.

"I have been trying to contact you," he said, struggling to disentangle the bundle of whisk brooms, hairbrushes, feather dusters, toilet brushes so he could drop them on the floor. "You have had the letters, the messages."

"I don't want to see you. I've done what you want, you have the film. So stop bothering me." She turned and put her hand on the knob.

"Don't do that!" he shouted, sending the last brush clattering against the wall. He groped in his inner jacket pocket and found his glasses. Putting them on he drew himself up, became calmer. "The films are valueless."

"You mean they didn't come out? I'm sure I did everything right."

"Not technically, that's not what I'm talking about. The notebook, the equations—they had nothing to do with the Daleth effect. They are all involved with Rasmussen's fusion generator and not what we want at all."

Martha tried not to smile—but she was glad somehow. She had done as she had been asked, and she had struck out. It was not her fault about the notebook.

"Well, can't you steal the fusion generator? Isn't that valuable too?"

"This is not a matter of commercial value," Baxter told her coldly, a good deal of his old manner restored. "In any case the fusion unit is being patented, we can license the rights. What you and I are concerned with is national security, nothing less than that."

He glared at her, and she pulled the edges of her housecoat more tightly around her.

"There's nothing more I can do for you. Everything is on the Moon now, you know that. Arnie's gone too—"

"I'll tell you what you can do, and there's not much time left. Do you think I would have gone out on a limb with this rig if things were not vital?"

"You do look sort of foolish," she said, and tried not to giggle.

Baxter gave her a look of pure, uncut hatred, and it took him a moment to control himself. "Now you listen to me," he finally said. "You're going to the ceremony today, and you will be going aboard the ship afterward and there are things we need to know about it. I want you to—"

"I'll do nothing for you. You can leave now."

Martha reached for the doorknob as he took her by the upper arm, his fingers sinking in like steel hooks. She gasped with pain as he dragged her away from it, pulling her up close to him, speaking into her face from inches away. *His breath smells of Sen-Sen*, she thought. *I didn't know they still made it*. She was ready to cry, her arm hurt so much.

"Listen you, you are going to do like I say. If you want a reason other than loyalty to your country—just remember that I have a roll of film from your camera with your fingerprints all over it, and pictures of your floor. The Danes would love to see that, wouldn't they?"

His smile made her think of a rictus, the kind that was supposed to be on people's faces when they died of pain. She disengaged her arm from his grasp and stepped back. It would be a complete waste to tell this man what she thought of him.

"What do you want me to do?" she asked finally, looking at the floor as she said it.

"That's more like it. You're a great camera addict, so take this brooch. Pin it onto your purse before you go."

She held it in her palm; it was not unattractive and would go well with her black alligator. A large central stone was surrounded by a circle of diamond chips and what could be small rubies. It was finished in hand-chased gold, rimmed by ornate whorls.

"Point your purse and press here," he said, indicating the top whorl. "It's wide angle, the opening is preset, it will work in almost any light. There are over a hundred shots in here so be generous. I want pictures of the bridge and the engine room if you get there, close-ups of the controls, shots of hallways, stairs, doors, compartments, airlocks. Everything. Later on I will show you prints and you will be asked to describe what they are, so take close notice of everything and the sequence of your visit through the ship."

"I don't know anything about this kind of work. Can't you get someone else, please? There will be hundreds there. . . ."

"If we had anyone else—do you think we would be asking

you?'' The last word was spoken with cold contempt, thrown at her as he bent to pick up the brushes. He shook a dishmop in her direction.

"And don't go making little accidents like dropping it, or breaking it, or exposing all the film in the dark and blaming us. I know all the tricks. You have no choice. You will take the pictures as I have told you. Here, this is for you." He handed her a brush, smiling coldly, sure of himself. He opened the door and was gone.

Martha looked down at it—then hurled it from her. Yes, that's what he thought. A toilet brush. She was shaking as she went to finish dressing.

* * *

"Look at the crowds!" Ove said, steering around a busload of cheering students who were waving flags from all the windows.

"Can you blame them?" Ulla asked. She was sitting in the back of the car with Martha. "This is certainly a wonderful day."

"Weather too," Ove said, glancing up at the sky. "Plenty of clouds, but no rain. No sun—but you can't have everything."

Martha sat silently, clutching her purse, the big gold brooch prominent on the flap. Ulla had noticed it, and she had had to make up a quick lie.

It would have been impossible to get close to the waterfront if they had not had their official invitation. They were waved through the barriers, and directed to Amalienborg Palace, where the immense square had been sectioned off for parking. From there it was a short walk down Larsens Plads to the water's edge. There was a holiday air even here, with a band playing lustily, bunting flapping on the stands erected on the dock, the guests nodding to each other as they took their places.

"Ten minutes," Ove said looking at his watch. "We had better hurry. Unless Martha thinks her husband will be late?"

"Nils!"

They all laughed at the thought, Martha along with the others. For seconds at a time she would feel right at home here, being ushered to her seat—not ten feet from the King and the Royal Family—smiling happily at friends. Then memory would return with a sinking in her midriff, and she would clutch at her purse, sure that people were looking at it. Then the band broke into "King Christian," the Royal Anthem, and there was a great rustling as everyone rose. After that the National Anthem, "There Is a Lovely Land," terminating with a great flourish on the drums. The last notes died away and they sat down, and at almost the same instant a distant whistling sound could be heard. They all looked up, shielding their eyes, trying to see. The sound deepened, turned to a rumble, and a dark speck broke through the layer of clouds high above.

"Right on time, to the second!" Ove said, excited.

With startling suddenness the dot grew, enlarged to giant proportions, appearing to fall straight toward them. There were gasps from the audience, and a choked-off scream.

The speed slowed, more and more, until the great shape was drifting down as softly as a falling feather, dropping toward the still water of the Inderhavn before them. There were more gasps as its true size became obvious. The great white and black hull was as big as any ocean-going ship, thousands of tons of dead weight. Falling. There was something unbelievable about its presence in the air before them. An immense disk, a half a city block long, flat on top and bottom, with the windowed bulge of the bridge protruding from the leading edge. It had no obvious means of propulsion; there was no sound other than the air rushing around its flanks.

Absolute silence gripped the onlookers, so hushed that the cries of the seagulls could be clearly heard. The great ship came to a complete halt, airborne, a few meters above the water. Then, with infinite precision, it dropped lower. Easing its tremendous bulk into the water so carefully that only a single small wave eased out to slap against the face of the wharf. As it moved closer, hatches opened on its upper decks and men brought out lines to secure it.

A spontaneous cheer broke out as the onlookers surged to their feet, shouting at the top of their lungs, clapping, the enthusiastic music of the band drowned out by their joyous noise. Martha shouted along with the others, everything else forgotten in the wild happiness of the moment.

In strong black letters, picked out against the white, the ship's name could be clearly read. *Holger Danske*. The proudest name in Denmark.

Even before the lines were secured, a passenger ramp was pushed out to the opened entrance. A small knot of officials was waiting to welcome the officers who strode down to them. Even at this distance Nils's great form was clearly visible among the others. They saluted, shook hands, and came forward to the reviewing stand. Nils passed close enough to smile when Martha waved.

After that there were honors and awards, a few brief words from the King, some longer speeches from the politicians. It was the Prime Minister who made the official pronouncement. He stood for a long moment, the wind whipping free strands of his hair, looking at the great ship before him. When he spoke, there was a heartfelt sincerity in his words.

"In the old legend, Holger Danske lies sleeping, ready to wake and come to Denmark's aid when she is in need. During the war the resistance movement took the name Holger Danske, and it was used with honor. Now we have a vessel by that name, the first of many, that will aid Denmark in a way no one ever suspected.

"We are opening up the solar system to mankind. This accomplishment is so grand that it is almost beyond imagining. I like to think about the seas of space as another ocean to be crossed the way Danish seafarers crossed in the nineteenth century, with new and fantastic lands on the other side. Science shall profit, from the observatory and the cryogenic laboratories now being built on the Moon. Industry shall profit, from the new sources of raw materials waiting for us out there. Mankind shall profit, because this is a joint venture of all the nations of the world. It is our fondest hope that the cause of peace shall profit—because out there, in space, our world is small and veiled and far away. Looking from there it is hard to see the separate continents, while national boundaries are completely invisible. Vital evidence that we are one world, one mankind.

"Denmark is too small a country to even attempt to exploit an entire solar system—even if we so wished. We do not. We eagerly seek the cooperation of the entire world. In two days *Holger Danske* will leave on the first voyage to Mars with representatives of many nations aboard. Scientific facilities are under construction there, and scientific workers from a great many countries will remain behind on the red planet to begin a number of research projects. The political representatives will return to tell the people in their own countries what the future will be like. It will be a good one. As Danes we are proud to be able to bring it about."

He sat down to a thunderous applause, and the band played. The television cameras took in everything while the announcement was made that the guests could now visit the spaceship.

"Wait until you see it," Ove said. "The first ship ever designed for this job—and no expense has been spared. It is basically a cargo ship, but the fact is well disguised. The entire interior section is made up of cargo holds, with the operating compartments of the ship forward. Which leaves all of the outside for cabins. Each one with a porthole. Luxury, I tell you. Come on, before the press gets too heavy."

Entrance to the ship was through the customs hall that was used when the Oslo ferry normally tied up at this pier. And the customs officers were still there—still doing their usual jobs. No packages were allowed aboard, briefcases and containers were being checked in. With utmost politeness, the men who were boarding were asked to show the contents of their pockets, the women turned out their handbags. There might be complaints, but high-ranking police and Army officers stood by to handle them quietly. There were even an admiral and a general, chatting with a departmental minister and an ambassador, in a small room to one side. The theory was obviously to have someone of equal—or greater—rank to handle any complaints.

There were none. A few raised eyebrows and cold looks at first, but the Prime Minister led the way by turning out his pockets and showing the contents of his wallet. It had obviously been staged that way, but was important nevertheless. The safety of the *Holger Danske* was not to be compromised.

As the line moved forward slowly, Martha Hansen found herself paralyzed with fear. She would be discovered and disgraced, and if there had been any place to run to she would have gone at once. But, stumbling, she could only follow the others. Ulla was saying something, and she could only nod dumbly in answer. Then she was at the counter and a tall, stern-faced customs officer was facing her. He slowly reached his hand out.

"This is a great day for your husband, Fru Hansen," he said. "Might I . . . ?" He gestured toward her purse. She extended it.

"If you will just open it," he said.

She did so, and he poked through it.

"Your compact," he said, pointing. She handed it to him and he snapped it open, and returned it.

The glittering eye of the camera brooch pointed directly at him. For a long moment he looked at it, smiling.

"That is all, thank you." And he turned away.

The Rasmussens were waiting, and Nils was waving from the deck above. She raised her hand, waved back. They went aboard.

Martha held her purse before her, one finger on her new brooch, wondering what she would say to Nils if he noticed it. She need not have worried about it. Normally the calmest of men while on duty, he was not so today. He had his hands clasped behind his back—perhaps to calm them—but his eyes were bright with excitement.

"Martha, this is the day!" he said, embracing her, lifting her free of the deck for a moment while he kissed her. With passion. She was dizzy when he put her down.

"My goodness . . ." she said.

"Have you seen this giant of a barge? Isn't she a dream? There has been nothing like it since the world began. We could carry poor little *Blaeksprutten* as a lifeboat, honestly! The best part is that this is not a makeshift or a compromise, but a vessel designed only for use with the Daleth drive. My bridge is right out in the leading edge for lateral movement, just like an aircraft, yet has full visibility both up and down for acceleration. Come on—let me show it to you. All except the engine room, that's locked up while visitors are aboard. And if we had the time I would damn well show you my bedroom as well as my cabin." He put his arm about her as they walked. "Martha, after flying this beauty everything is changed. I think now that flying the biggest aircraft would be like, I don't know, like pedaling a kiddy car. Come on!"

As they walked through the open spacelock her finger touched the golden whorl on her brooch and she felt it depress slightly.

She hated herself.

22

HOLGER DANSKE

"Aren't they all aboard yet?" Arnie asked, looking out at the wharf from the high vantage point of the bridge. Two men came out of the customs shed, bending over and holding their homburgs down with their hands as the Baltic wind whipped around them. The porters, with their suitcases, came after them.

"Not yet, but we should be nearing the end," Nils told him. "I'll check with the purser." He dialed the office in the entrance hallway, and the small telephone screen lit up with full color image of the chief purser.

"Sir?"

"How is your head count going?"

The purser consulted his charts, ticking them off with a pencil. "Six more passengers to go, and that's the lot."

"Thanks." He hung up. "Not too bad. Considering that they are doing everything but x-ray them and examine the fillings in their teeth. I suppose that I'll be hearing plenty of complaints. Ship captains never appear among the passengers until after the first day at sea. I think maybe I'll try that."

"With the new computer setup I imagine that you do not have to worry about your exact take-off time?"

"There's nothing to it." He patted the gray cabinet of the computer readout near his pilot's position. "I tell this thing when I want to leave and it gets the answer back almost before we're through typing. While we are in dock it is plugged into a direct land line to Moscow. After take-off our computer talks to theirs and there are constant course and velocity checks and corrections."

They watched another late arrival hurry across the wharf.

"Were the Americans upset about our using the Soviet computer?" Arnie asked.

"I suppose so, but they couldn't complain because we had no simple line connections to theirs. But we are using only U.S. spacesuits so it evens out. Done on purpose, I'm sure. How was Ove when you saw him?"

Arnie shrugged. "Still in bed, coughing like a seal, still with a fever. I waved from the door, he would not let me come in. He wished us the best of luck. The flu went to his chest."

"I'm glad you could take his place—though I'm sorry we had to ask you. As soon as all the bugs are ironed out we won't be needing physicists in the engine room anymore."

"I do not mind. In fact I enjoy it. Research and teaching are going to be very tame after some of these flights. Like *Blaeksprutten* to the Moon . . ."

"With the telephone box welded to the hull! God, those were the days. Look how far we have come." He waved around the expanse of the bridge, at the uniformed crewmen on duty. The radio operator, talking to control ashore, the navigator, second pilot, instrumentation operator, computer mate. It was an impressive sight. The phone sounded and he answered it.

"All passengers aboard, Captain."

"Fine. Prepare for take-off in ten minutes."

Arnie was in the engine room for take-off, and in all truth he found very little to do. The crewmen were respectful enough, but they knew their jobs well. The Daleth drive had been automated to the point where the computer monitored it, and human attention was almost redundant. And the same was true of the fusion generator. When Arnie was hungry he had some food sent in, although he knew that he had been invited to the first night banquet. That he would avoid, with good reason, since he loathed this kind of affair. He was only too glad to help out and to take Ove's place, when his friend was ill, but he did not really enjoy it. The laboratory at ***Manebasen*** interested him far more, the new line of research he had started, and the classes he held in Daleth theory for the technicians.

And then there were the passengers. He had the list, and it did not take too much honesty to admit that this was the real reason he stayed sealed in the operating section. He had found no friends or associates among the scientists, they were all second-rate people for the most part. Not second rate, that wasn't fair, but juniors—assistants to the important people. As though the universities of the world were not trusting their top minds to this unorthodox endeavor. Well, it did not matter. The young men could take observations as well as the old, and the raw facts and figures they returned with would have the others clamoring for a place on the next mission. Making a start, that was what counted.

As to the others, the politicians, he knew nothing about them. There were very few names he had ever heard before. But then, he was not the most careful of political observers. Probably all second consuls and that sort of thing, trying the water temperature this first trip so their betters could take a plunge later on.

But he knew one politician. He must face the fact—this was why he was staying away from the passenger section. But what good was it doing? General Avri Gev was aboard and he would have to meet him sooner or later. Arnie looked at his watch. Why not now? They would all be full of good food and drink. Perhaps he would catch Avri in a good mood. Knowing that this was impossible even as he thought it. But the entire voyage to Mars would take less than two days—and he was not going to spend all of the time skulking down here.

After checking with the technicians—no, everything was fine now, they would call him if there were any problems—he went to his cabin for his jacket, and then to the airtight doorway that led to the passenger section.

"Fine flight, sir," the master-at-arms said, saluting. He was an old soldier, a sergeant, obviously transferred from the Army with all his stripes and decorations. He looked at his television screen that showed the empty corridor beyond, then pressed the button that opened the door. There were airtight doors throughout the *Holger Danske*, but this was the only one that could not be opened from either side. Arnie nodded and went through, and found General Gev waiting for him around the first bend.

"I was hoping you would come out," Gev said. "If not I would put a call in for you."

"Good evening, Avri."

"Would you come to my cabin? I have some Scotch whisky I want you to try."

"I'm not much of a drinker . . ."

"Come anyway. Mr. Sakana gave it to me."

Arnie stared at him, trying to read something from those impassive, tanned features. They had been talking in English. There was no one named Mr. Sakana. It was a Hebrew word meaning "danger."

"Well—if you insist."

Gev led the way, showing Arnie in, then locking the door behind him.

"What is wrong?" Arnie asked.

"In a moment. Hospitality first. Sit down, please, take that chair."

Like all of the cabins, this one was luxurious. The port, with the metal cover now automatically swung back after passing through the Van Allen belt, opened onto the stars of space. A hand-made Rya rug was on the floor. The walls were paneled with teak and decorated with Sikker Hansen prints. The furnitute was Scandinavian modern.

"And color television in every cabin," Gev said, pointing to the large screen where cannon fired silently in a battle scene from the new film *From Atlanta to the Sea*. He took a bottle from the bar.

"It is practical," Arnie said. "As well as furnishing entertainment from taped programs. It is part of the telephone system as well. Did you get me here to talk about interior decorating?"

"Not really. Here, try this. Glen Grant, pure malt, unblended, twelve years old. I developed a taste for it while I served with the British. There is something wrong aboard this ship. *Lehayim*."

"What do you mean?" Arnie held his drink, puzzled.

"Just taste it. A thousand percent better than that filthy slivovitz you used to serve. I mean just that. Wrong. There are at least two men among the Eastern delegation whom I recognized. They are thugs, known agents, criminals."

"You are sure?"

"Of course. Have you forgotten that I am charged with internal security? I read all the Interpol reports."

"What could they be doing here?" Abstracted, he took too big a drink and started coughing.

"Sip it. Like mother's milk. I don't *know* what they are doing here, but I can readily guess. They are after the Daleth drive."

"That is impossible!"

"Is it?" Gev managed to look cynically amused and depressed at the same time. "Might I ask you what kind of security precautions have been taken?" Arnie was silent, and Gev laughed.

"So don't tell me. I don't blame you for being suspicious. But I do not make a very good army of one, and the only other Israeli aboard is that round-shouldered *shlub* of a biologist. A genius he is supposed to be, a fighting man he is not."

"You were not this friendly the last time we talked."

"With good reason, as you well know. But times have changed and Israel is making the best of what she has. We don't have your Daleth drive—though at least it has a good Hebrew name—but the Danes are being far more accommodating than we ever expected. They admit that a lot of the Daleth theory was developed in Israel, therefore are giving us first priority in scientific and commercial exploitation. We are even going to have our own base on the Moon. Right now there is nothing to really complain about. We still want the Daleth drive, but at the moment we don't intend to shoot anyone for it. I want to talk to Captain Hansen."

Arnie chewed his lip, concentrating, then finished the rest of the whisky without even realizing it. "Stay here," he finally said. "I will tell him what you have seen. He will call you."

"Don't be too long, Arnie," Gev said quietly. He was very serious.

* * *

Nils had made a short speech at the banquet, then retreated to the bridge pleading the charge of duty. He was sitting with one leg over the arm of his chair, looking at the stars. He spun about when Arnie told him what Gev had said.

"Impossible!"

"Perhaps. But I believe him."

"Could it be a trick of his own? To get to the bridge?"

"I don't know. I doubt it. He is a man of honor—and I believe him."

"I hope that you are right—and that he is wrong. But I can't just ignore his charges. I'll get him up, but the master-at-arms will be standing behind him all the time." He turned to the phone.

General Gev came at once. The sergeant walked two paces behind him with his drawn automatic pistol in his hand. He held it at his waist, where it could not be grabbed, and he looked ready to use it.

"Could I see your passenger list?" Gev asked, then went through it carefully.

"This one and this one," he said, underscoring their names. "They have different aliases in the files, but they are the same men. One is wanted for sabotage, the other is suspected in a bombing plot. Very nasty types."

"It is hard to believe," Nils said. "They are the accredited representatives of these countries. . . ."

"Who do exactly whatever Mother Russia asks them to. Please don't be naïve, Captain Hansen. A satellite means just that. Bought and paid for and ready to dance when someone else whistles the tune."

The telephone burred at Nils's elbow and he switched it on automatically.

A man's frightened face appeared on the screen, bright blood running down his face.

"Help!" he screamed.

Then there was a loud noise and the screen went blank.

23

"What compartment was that?" Nils shouted, reaching for the dial on the phone. "Did anyone recognize that man?"

Gev reached out and stopped him as he was about to dial: the sergeant raised his gun and centered it on Gev's back.

"Wait," Gev said. "Think. There is trouble, you know that much. That is enough for the moment. Alert your defenses first—if you have any. Then find out what area is threatened. I saw airtight doors throughout the ship. Can they be closed from here?"

"Yes . . ."

"Then close them. Slow down whatever is happening."

Nils hesitated an instant. "It's a good idea, sir," the sergeant said. Nils nodded.

"Close all interior bulkhead doorways," he ordered. The instrumentation officer threw back a protective plastic cover and flipped a row of switches.

"Those doors can be opened on the spot," the sergeant said.

"The local controls can be overridden in an emergency," the instrumentation officer said.

"This is an emergency," Nils told him. "Do it."

Gev went to the wall by the door, out of their way. The sergeant lowered his gun.

"I did not mean to interfere with your command, Captain," Gev said. "It is just that I have a certain experience in these things."

"I'm glad that you're here," Nils told him. "We may have to use that experience." He dialed the engine room, and the call was answered at once by one of the technicians.

"A malfunction, sir. Exit doors are closed and can't be budged. . . ."

"This is an emergency. There is trouble aboard, we don't know quite what yet. Stay away from the doors, no one gets in there—and let me know if you have any trouble."

"I think I recognized that man," the radio operator said hesitantly. "A cook, or something to do with the kitchen."

"Good enough." Nils dialed the kitchen but the call was not completed. "That's where they are. But what the hell can they want with the kitchen?"

"Weapons, perhaps," Gev said. "Knives, cleavers, there will be plenty of them. Or perhaps something else . . . Could I see a plan of the ship?"

Nils turned to Arnie. "Tell me quickly," he said. "Is this man on our side?"

Arnie nodded slowly. "I think he is now."

"All right. Sergeant, back to your post. Neergaard, get me the deck plans."

They unrolled them on the table and Gev stabbed down with his finger. "Here, what does *kokken* mean?"

"Kitchen."

"It makes sense. Look. It can be reached from the dining room, unlike any other part of the working section of this ship. Also—it shares an interior wall with the engine room. Which I assume is this one here."

Nils nodded.

"Then they won't try the doors. They'll cut their way in. Is there any way you can reach the engine room quickly? To reinforce the people there in case . . ."

The phone rang and the engineering officer came on the screen. "A torch of some kind, Captain, burning a hole through the wall. What should we do?"

"What did he say?" Gev asked, catching the man's worried tone but not understanding the Danish. Arnie quickly explained. Gev touched Nils's arm. "Tell them to get a bench or a table against the wall at this spot, pile anything heavy against it. Make entrance as difficult as possible."

Nils was looking haggard after issuing the orders. "They can't possibly stop them from breaking in."

"Reinforcements?"

There was no humor in Nils's smile. "We have one gun aboard, the one worn by the sergeant."

"If possible get him to the engine room. Unless you can counterattack through the kitchen. Strike hard, it is the only way."

"You would know," Nils said. "Get the sergeant in here. I'll have to ask him to volunteer. It's almost suicide."

The sergeant nodded when they told him what was happening.

"I'll be happy to undertake this, Captain. It could work if they are not heavily armed. I have another clip of bullets, but I won't take them. I doubt if there will be much chance to reload. I'll make these count. I can go in through that door from the aft storeroom. If it opens quietly enough I could surprise them."

He carefully laid his cap aside and turned to General Gev, tapping the row of decorations on his chest. Instead of Danish he talked English now, with a thick Cockney accent.

"I saw you looking at this, General. You're right, I was in Palestine, in the British Army, fighting the Hun. But when they started on your refugee ships afterwards, keeping them out, I went lost. Deserted. Back to Denmark. That wasn't my kind of thing."

"I believe you, Sergeant. Thank you for telling me."

The doors were unlocked in sequence so he could go through.

"He should be there by now," Nils said. "Call the engine room."

The technician was excited. "Captain—it sounded like shots! We could hear them through the wall, an awful lot of them. And the cutting has stopped."

"Good," Gev said when he was told what had happened. "They may not have been stopped but they have been slowed down."

"The sergeant has not come back," Nils said.

"He did not expect to." There was no expression at all on General Gev's face: emotion in battle was a luxury he could not afford. "Now a second counterattack must be launched. More men, volunteers if possible. Arm them with anything. We have a moment's respite and advantage must be taken of it. I will lead them if you will permit me. . . ."

"The phone, Captain," the radio operator said. "It is one of the American delegation."

"I can't be bothered now."

"He says he knows about the attack and he wants to help."

Nils picked up the phone, and the image of a man with thick-rimmed glasses, his face set in lines of gloom, looked out at him.

"I understand the Reds are attacking you, Captain Hansen. I can offer you some help. We are on the way to the bridge now."

"Who are you? How do you know this?"

"My name is Baxter. I'm a security officer. I was sent on this voyage just in case something like this happened. I have some armed men with me, we're on our way now."

Nils did not need to see General Gev shake his head *no* to make up his mind.

"Did you say *armed* men? No arms were permitted aboard this ship."

"Armed for your defense, Captain. And you will need us now."

"I do not. Stay where you are. Someone will come to collect your weapons."

"We're leaving for the bridge now. Our country has stepped in before in a war; don't forget that. And NATO—"

"Damn NATO and damn you! If you make one move towards this bridge you are no different from those others."

"There have been quislings before, Captain Hansen," Baxter said, sternly. "Your government will appreciate what we are doing even if you don't." He broke the connection.

Gev was already running toward the exit to the passenger section of the ship. "It's locked," he shouted back. "Is there any way we can reinforce this door?"

The others led by Nils, were close behind him. They were just in time to stare, aghast, at the television monitor. A group of men, five, ten, came into sight around the bend in the corridor outside, racing toward the door. Baxter was in front and behind him ran one of the Formosa delegates, some South Americans, a Vietnamese. One of them raised a broken-off chair leg and swung at the camera. It went blank.

"This is going to be difficult," Gev said calmly, looking at the door. "We are going to have to fight on two fronts—and we are not even equipped for combat on one."

"Captain," the radio operator called from the bridge. "Engine room reports that the cutting has started again."

There was a deep boom of an explosion, ear-hurting loud in the confined corridor, and the door bulged toward them, twisted and a great cloud of smoke boiled in. They were stunned, knocked down. Then the door shivered and moved further inward, and a man holding a makeshift gun began to squeeze through.

Gev sprang, hands out. Grabbing the man's wrist, twisting it so the gun pointed to the ceiling. It fired once, an almost soundless splat to their numbed ears. Then Gev chopped down with the edge of his free hand, breaking the man's neck. He fumbled an instant with the unusual mechanism of the gun, then poked it through the opening over the dead man's back and fired until it was empty.

This only delayed the attackers a moment. Then the door was pushed wider and two men climbed in, treading on the corpse. Nils hit one in the face with his fist, knocking him back through the opening with its force.

But they were outnumbered—and outgunned. Yet they gave a very good accounting of themselves. General Gev did not drop until he was hit with at least three bullets. They did not shoot Nils, but men hung from him, holding down his arms, while another clubbed him into submission. Arnie knew nothing about fighting, though he tried with very little success. Dead and wounded were left behind when they were dragged back to the bridge. The radio operator, the only crewman remaining there, was talking on the radio.

"Shut up." Baxter shouted at him, raising his gun. "Who are you talking to?"

The operator, white-faced, clutched the microphone. "It is our Moon base. They have relayed the call to Copenhagen. I told them what was happening here. The others have broken into the engine room, taken it."

Baxter thought for a long moment, then lowered the gun and smiled. "You've done all right. Continue your report. Tell them that you have received assistance. The commies are not getting away with this. Now—how do I get in touch with the engine room?"

The radio operator pointed silently at the telephone screen, where an impassive face looked out. Baxter was just as unemotional as he strode over to the phone.

"You're a traitor, Schmidt," he said. "I knew that as soon as I saw you were a member of the East German delegation. That was not very wise of you." Baxter turned to Nils who had been placed in a chair. He was struggling back to consciousness. "I know this man, Captain. A paid informer. It's a good thing for you that I am here."

General Gev slumped on the floor against the wall, listening silently, apparently unaware of his blood-soaked, dripping leg. His right arm had been hit by a bullet as well, and he had his hand pushed into the open front of his shirt. Arnie's glasses were broken, gone, and he blinked myopically, trying to understand what was happening.

Baxter looked distastefully at Schmidt's image. "I don't enjoy dealing with traitors. . . ."

"We all have to make small sacrifices." Schmidt's words were heavy with irony. Baxter flushed with anger but went on, ignoring them.

"There seems to be a stalemate here. We hold the bridge and the controls."

"While I and my men are in charge of the engines and the drive unit. My forces are not as strong as they should be—but we are well armed. I think that you will find it impossible to defeat us. You will not get us out of here. So what do you intend to do, Mr. Baxter?"

"Is Dr. Nikitin with you?"

"Of course! Why else do you think we are here?"

Baxter broke the connection and turned to Nils. "This is very bad, Captain."

"What are you talking about?" The fog was clearing somewhat from Nils's battered head. "Who is this Nikitin?"

"One of their better physicists," Arnie said. "With the diagrams and circuitry he should know the basic principles of the Daleth drive by now."

"Exactly," Baxter said and put his gun away. "They hold the engine room, but cannot take the bridge, so all is not lost. Report that to your superiors," he ordered the radio operator.

"It is a stalemate for the moment—but if we had not been here they would have taken the entire ship. You see, Captain, you were mistaken about us."

"Where did you get the guns?" Nils asked. "That explosive?"

"Of what importance is that? Gun barrels looking like fountain pens, swallowed ammunition, plastic explosive in toothpaste tubes. The usual thing. It's not important."

"It is to me," Nils said, sitting up straighter. "And what do you propose to do now, Mr. Baxter?"

"Hard to say. Bandage you people up first. Try to arrange a deal with that double-agent Kraut. We'll work something out. Have to turn back, I guess. Prevent any more killing. They know about the drive now, so the cat is out of the bag. No secrets left between allies, hey? Your people in Copenhagen will understand. I imagine America will handle it through NATO, but that's not my area of responsibility. I'm just the man in the field. But you can be sure of one thing." He drew himself up. "There is going to be no Daleth gap. The Russians are not going to get ahead of us with this one."

Nils rose slowly, painfully, and stumbled to his chair at the controls. "Who are you talking to?" he asked the radio operator.

"There is a patch to Copenhagen. One of the Minister's assistants. It is the middle of the night there and the others were asleep when I called. The King, the Prime Minister, they're on the way."

"I'm afraid we can't wait for them." They spoke English so Baxter could understand. Nils now turned to him. "I would like to explain what has happened."

"By all means, sure. They'll want to know."

Still in English, slowly and carefully, Nils outlined the recent occurrences. After a long delay, while the signal reached out to Earth and the answer came back, the man at the other end spoke in Danish, and Nils answered in the same language. When he had finished, there was a tense silence on the bridge.

"Well?" Baxter asked. "What was that about? What did they say?"

"They agreed with me," Nils told him. "The situation is hopeless."

"Good thinking."

"We agreed on what must be done. He thanked us."

"What the *hell* are you talking about?"

Nils was finished with patience and formality now. He spat the words with a slow anger that had finally burned through.

"I'm talking about stopping you, little man. Violence, death, killing—that is all you know. I don't see an ounce of difference between you and your paid creatures here, and that swine now in charge of the engine room. In the name of good you do evil. For national pride you would destroy mankind. When will you admit that all men are brothers—and then find some way to stop killing your brothers? Your country alone has enough atomic bombs to blow up the world four times over. So why must you add the additional destruction of the Daleth effect?"

"The Russkies—"

"Are the same as you. From where I am, here in space, about to die, I can't tell the difference."

"Die?" Baxter was frightened, he raised his gun again.

"Yes. Did you think we would just hand you the Daleth drive? We tried to keep it away from you without killing, but you forced this on us. There are at least five tons of explosive distributed about the frame of this ship. Actuated by radio signal from Earth . . ."

A series of rapid musical notes was sounding from the speaker and Baxter screamed hoarsely, turning, firing at the controls, hitting the radio operator, emptying his gun into the banks of instruments.

"A radio signal that cannot be interrupted form here."

Nils turned to Arnie who was standing quietly. Nils took his hand and started to say something. General Gev was laughing, victoriously, enjoying this cosmic jest. The rightness appealed to him. Baxter shouted . . .

With a single great burst of flame everything ended.

24

MOON BASE

For Martha Hansen, events had a dreamlike quality that made them bearable. It had started when Ove had called that night, 4:17 in the morning, her clearest recollection of his call had been the position of the glowing hands in the dark while his voice buzzed in her ear.

4:17. The numbers must mean something important because they kept coming to the front of her mind. Was that the time her world had ended? No, she was still very much alive. But Nils was away on one of his flights. He had always returned from his flights before this. . . .

That was the point where her thoughts would always slide around and come to something else. 4:17. The people who had called, talked to her, the Prime Minister himself. The Royal Family . . . 4:17. She had at least learned to be polite in finishing school, if she had not learned anything else.

But she should have noticed more about the trip to the Moon. But even then the numbness had prevailed. They had flown in one of the new Moon ships, space-buses they were being called. Very much like flying in a jet, only with more room all around. A long cabin, rows of seats, sandwiches and drinks. Even a hostess. A tall ash-blond girl who had seemed to stay quite close for most of the trip, had even talked to her a bit. With the kind of lilting Swedish accent the men loved. But sad now, like all of them. When had she seen a smile last?

The funeral ceremony had seemed empty. There was the monument all right, in the airless soil just beyond the windows. Draped in flags, a bugle had wailed a plaintive call that pulled at the heartstrings. But no one was buried there. No one would ever be buried there. An explosion, they had told her. Died instantly, painless. And so far away. Days later Ove Rasmussen had told her the real story behind the explosion. It sounded like madness. People did not really do this kind of thing to each other. But they did. And Nils was the kind of man who could do what he had done. It wasn't suicide, she could not imagine Nils committing suicide. But a victory for what he knew was right. If he had to die at the same time she knew he would consider this second, and not give it much consideration at all. In dying he had taught her things about the man, living, that she had never realized.

"Just a drop of sherry?" Ulla asked, bending over her with a glass in her hand. They were in a lounge, the ceremony was over. They would be returning to Copenhagen soon.

"Yes, please. Thank you."

Martha sipped the drink and tried to pay attention to the others. She knew she had not been doing this of late, and also knew that they had been making allowances for it. She did not like that. It was too much like being pitied. She sipped again, and looked around. There was a high-ranking Army officer at the table with them, and someone—she forgot his name—from the Ministry of Space.

"It won't happen again,"Ove said angrily. "We treated the other countries as if they were civilized, not monsters of what?—national greed, that is the only term for it. Smuggled weapons, hired thugs, subversion, piracy in space. Almost unbelievable. They won't have a second chance. And we are not going to kill ourselves any more. We'll kill them if they ask for it."

"Hear, hear," the Army officer said.

"The new Daleth ships will be built with a complete internal division. We'll advertise the fact. Crew on one side, passengers on the other, without as much as a bulkhead in between. We'll have a troop of soldiers aboard if needs be. Armed with guns, gas . . ."

"Let's not get carried away, old boy."

"Yes, of course. But you know what I mean. It can't ever happen again."

"They won't stop trying." the man from the Ministry said gloomily. "So they'll probably get the drive from us some day, if they don't stumble onto it themselves first."

"Fine," Ove said. "But we'll put that day off as long as possible. What else can we do?"

Silence was the only answer to this. What else *could* they do?

"Excuse me," Martha said, and the men rose as she left. She knew where to find the commanding officer of the base, and he was most accommodating.

"Of course, Mrs. Hansen," he told her. "There is no cause at all to refuse a request like this. We'll of course take care of sending Captain Hansen's effects back to you. But if there is anything you wish to take now . . ."

"No, it's not that so much. I just want to see where he lived when he was here. I hardly saw him at all this last year."

"Quite understandable. If you will permit me, I'll take you there myself."

It was a small room, not luxurious, in one of the first sections that had been built. She was left alone there. The walls, under their coats of paint, still showed the grain of the wooden mold the cement had been poured into. The bed was metal framed and hard, the wardrobe and built-in drawers functional. The only note of luxury was a window that faced out upon the lunar plain. It was a porthole, really, one of the first jury-rigs. Two standard ship's portholes that had been welded together to make a double-thick window. She looked out at the airless reaches and the hills, sharp and clear beyond, and could imagine him standing here like this. His extra uniforms were hung neatly in the closet and she missed him, how she missed him! She still had tears left, not many, and she dabbed at her eyes with her handkerchief. It had been a mistake coming here, he was dead and gone and would never return to her. It was time to leave. As she turned to go she noticed the framed picture of her on the little desk. Small, in color, in a bathing suit, laughing during some happier time. For some reason she did not want to look at it. It was here because he had loved her, she knew that. She should always have known that. Despite everything.

Martha started to put the picture into her purse, but she did not really want it. She opened the top drawer of the dresser and poked it down under his pajamas. Her hand brushed something hard, and she pulled out a paperbound booklet. *Elementaer Vedligeholdelse og Drift af Daleth Maskinkomponenter Af Model IV* it was labeled, and as she mentally translated the compound, technical Danish terms, she flipped through the book. Diagrams, drawings, and equations flicked past as the meaning of the title registered in her brain.

Basic Maintenance and Operation of Daleth Drive Units Mark IV.

He must have been studying it; he always had to know all the details of the planes he flew. The new ships would be no different. He had stuffed it in here, forgotten it.

Men had died to obtain what she held in her hand. Other men had died to stop them.

She began to put it back into the drawer, then hesitated, looking at it again.

Baxter was dead, she had been told about that, dead aboard the ship. There was a new man at the embassy who had been trying to contact her, she had his name written down somewhere.

She could give this booklet to them and they would leave her alone. Everything would be settled once and for all and there would be no trouble.

Martha dropped the booklet into her purse and snapped it shut. It made no bulge at all. She slid the bureau drawer shut, looked around the room once more, then left.

When she rejoined the others some of them were already getting ready to leave. She glanced about the reception hall, seeking a familiar face. She found him, standing against the far wall, looking out of the large window.

"Herr Skou," she said, and he turned about sharply.

"Ah, Mrs. Hansen. I saw you, but I have not had a chance to talk to you. Everything, everything . . ."

He had a haunted look on his face, and she wondered if he, somehow, blamed himself for what had happened.

"Here," she said, opening her purse and handing him the booklet. "I found this with my husband's things. I didn't think that you wanted it lying around."

"Good God, no!" he said when he saw the title. "Thank you, most kind, helpful. People never think. Doesn't help my work, I tell you. Numbered copy, we thought it was on board the *Holger Danske*. I never realized." He drew himself up and made a short, formal bow.

"Thank you, Frau Hansen. I don't think you realize how helpful you have been."

She smiled. "But I do know, Herr Skou. My husband and many others died to preserve what is in that book. Could I do less? And it is the other way around. Until now, I don't think I realized how helpful you, everyone, has been to me."

And then it was time to return to Earth.

25

RUNGSTED KYST

The brakes in the Sprite were locked hard as it turned into the driveway, the tires squealing as it slid to a bucking stop. Ove Rasmussen jumped over the car door without opening it and ran up the front steps to push hard on the doorbell. Even as the chimes were sounding over and over again inside, he tried the handle. The door was unlocked and he threw it open.

"Martha—where are you?" he shouted. "Are you here?"

He closed the door and listened. There was only the ticking of a clock. Then he heard the muffled sobbing from the living room. She was sprawled on the couch, her shoulders shaking with the hopeless, uncontrolled crying. The newspaper lay on the floor beside her.

"Ulla called me, I was at the lab all night," he said. "You sounded so bad on the phone that she was getting hysterical herself. I came at once. What happened . . . ?"

Then he saw the front page of the newspaper and knew the answer. He bent and picked it up and looked at the photograph that almost filled the front page. It showed an egg-shaped vehicle about the size of a small car that was floating a few meters above a crowd of gaping people. A smiling girl waved from the little cockpit, and on the front, between the headlights, the word *Honda* could plainly be seen. The craft had no obvious means of propulsion. The headline read JAPANESE REVEAL GRAVITY SCOOTER, and underneath, CLAIM NEW PRINCIPLE WILL REVOLUTIONIZE TRANSPORTATION.

Martha was sitting up now, dabbing at her eyes with a sodden handkerchief. Her face was red and puffy, her hair in a tangle.

"I had a sleeping pill," she said, almost choking on the words. "Twelve hours. I didn't hear the radio, anything. While I was getting my breakfast ready I brought in the paper. And there . . ." Her voice broke and she could only point. Ove nodded wearily and dropped into the armchair.

"Is it true?" she asked. "The Japanese have the Daleth drive?"

He nodded again. Her fingers flew to her face, her nails sank into the flesh and she shrieked the words.

"Wasted! All killed for nothing! The Japs already knew about the Daleth effect—they stole it. Nils, all of them, they died for nothing!"

"Easy," Ove said, and leaned forward to hold her shoulders, feeling her body shake as she cried in agony. "Tears can't bring him back, or any of the others."

"All that security . . . no good . . . the secret leaked out . . ."

"Security killed them all," Ove said, and his voice was as bleak as a winter midnight. "A stupid, stupid waste."

The bitterness of his words did what sympathy could not do; it reached Martha, shocked her. "What are you talking about?" she said, rubbing the tears from her eyes with the back of her hand.

"Just that." Ove looked at the newspaper with black hatred, then ground it with his foot. "We had no eternal secret, just a lead on the others. Arnie and I tried to tell security that, but they would never listen. Apparently only Nils and his top officers knew about the destruction charges in the ship. If Arnie or I had known we would have made a public stink and would have refused to fly in her. It is all a criminal waste, criminal stupidity."

"What does this mean?" She was frightened of his words.

"Just that. Only politicians and security agents believe in Secrets with a captial S. And maybe the people who read the spy novels about those imaginary stolen secrets. But mother nature has no secrets. Everything is right out where you can see it. Sometimes the answer is complex, or you have to know the right place to look before you find it. Arnie knew that, and that is one of the reasons he brought his discovery to Denmark. It could be developed faster here because we have the heavy industrial machinery to build the Daleth ships. But it was only a matter of time before everyone else caught up. Once they knew that there *was* a Daleth effect they would know just what they were looking for. We had two things in our favor. A number of physicists around the world knew that Arnie was doing gravity research. He corresponded with them and they read about his work in the journals. What they did not know was that his basic approach was wrong. He discovered that fact but never had time to publish results. The real discovery of the Daleth effect came about through the telemetry records of the solar flare. Those data readouts were distributed to the cooperating countries, and it was only a matter of time before the connection was tracked down. We had that time, almost two years of it, and it gave us the lead that we needed."

"Then the killings, the spies . . ."

"All waste. The secret of security is to never let the right hand know what the left hand is doing. A secret agency tries to steal the secret while other secret laboratories try to develop it. And once these agencies get rolling they are very hard to stop. It would be ironic if it were not so tragic. I have finally heard the entire story myself—I was up all night with the security people getting briefed on the whole story. Do you know how many countries already had a lead to the nature of the Daleth effect when the ship was blown up? I'll tell you. *Five*. The Japanese thought they were first and tried to apply for international patents. Their applications were turned down by four countries because earlier patent applications had been filed in these countries and held under government security. Germany and India were two of these countries."

"And the other two?" She gasped the words as though she already knew.

"America and the Soviet Union."

"No!"

"I'm sorry. It hurts me as much to say it as it does for you to hear it. Your husband, Arnie, my friends and colleagues died in that explosion. Wasted. ***Because the countries that caused it already knew the answer***. But since the information was top secret they could not tell other agencies or men in the field. But I no more hold them to blame than I do our own security, who wired the explosives into the ship in the first place. Nor do I blame any other country involved in the mess. It is just institutionalized paranoia. All security men are the same, drawn to the work by their own insecurities and fears. They may be sincere patriots, but their sickness is what makes them demonstrate their patriotism in this manner. This kind of person will never understand that when it is steamboat time you build steamboats, airplane time you build airplanes."

"I don't understand you." She wanted to cry now but

she could not; she was beyond tears.

"The story always repeats itself. As soon as the Japanese even *heard* about American radar during World War II they went to work on it. They developed the magnetron and other vital parts almost as soon as the Americans did. Only internal squabbling and the lack of production facilities kept them from making it operational. It was radar time. And now . . . now it is Daleth time."

Then there was a long silence. A cloud passed over the sun outside and the room darkened. Finally Martha spoke: she had to ask the question.

"Was it all a waste? Their deaths. A complete waste?"

"No." Ove hesitated and tried to smile, but he could not do it. "At least I hope that it is not a complete waste. Men from a lot of countries died in that explosion. The shock of this could drive some sense into people's heads, and maybe even into politicians' heads. They might use this discovery for the mutual good of all mankind. Do the right thing just this once. Without bickering. Without turning it into one more fantastically destructive weapon. Used correctly the Daleth effect could make the world a paradise. The Japanese even went us one better—they've eliminated the separate power source. They looked into the energy conservation and found out that they could use the Daleth effect to power itself. So we now all live in the suburbs of the same world city. That fact will take some getting used to. But the world, all of us, must get together and face that fact. Any person or country who tries to use this power for harm or for war will have to be stopped—instantly—for the greater good of all.

"Look at it that way and the deaths are not a waste. If we can learn something from their sacrifice it might all have been worthwhile."

"Can we?" Martha asked. "Can we really? Make the kind of world we all say that we want but never seem able to attain?"

"We are going to have to," he said, leaning forward and taking her hands. "Or we will certainly die trying."

She laughed. Without humor.

"One world or none. I seem to have heard that before."

The cloud passed and the sun came out again, but inside the house, in the room where the two people sat, there was a darkness that would not lift.

JOURNEY THROUGH TIME AND SPACE

THE CITY OUTSIDE THE WORLD (03549-2—$1.50)
by Lin Carter

MIRKHEIM (03596-4—$1.50)
by Poul Anderson

NIGHT OF LIGHT (03366-X—$1.50)
by Philip Jose Farmer

TELEMPATH (03548-4—$1.50)
by Spider Robinson

WHIPPING STAR (03504-2—$1.50)
by Frank Herbert

THE WORLDS OF FRANK HERBERT (03502-6—$1.75)
by Frank Herbert

Send for a *free* list of all our books in print

These books are available at your local bookstore, or send price indicated plus 30¢ per copy to cover mailing costs to

Berkley Publishing Corporation
390 Murray Hill Parkway
East Rutherford, New Jersey 07073

CONAN
THE GREATEST SWORD AND SORCERY HERO OF THEM ALL!

THE HOUR OF THE DRAGON (03608-1—$1.95)
by Robert E. Howard

THE PEOPLE OF THE BLACK CIRCLE (03609-X—$1.95)
by Robert E. Howard

RED NAILS (03610-3—$1.95)
by Robert E. Howard

ALMURIC (03483-6—$1.95)
by Robert E. Howard

Send for a *free* list of all our books in print

These books are available at your local bookstore, or send price indicated plus 30¢ per copy to cover mailing costs to
Berkley Publishing Corporation
390 Murray Hill Parkway
East Rutherford, New Jersey 07073

THE CLASSIC SCIENCE FICTION OF ROBERT HEINLEIN

FARNHAM'S FREEHOLD	(03568-9—$1.95)
GLORY ROAD	(03783-5—$1.95)
THE MOON IS A HARSH MISTRESS	(03436-4—$1.75)
ORPHANS OF THE SKY	(03217-5—$1.25)
THE PAST THROUGH TOMORROW	(03178-0—$2.75)
PODKAYNE OF MARS	(03434-8—$1.50)
STARSHIP TROOPERS	(03218-3—$1.50)
STRANGER IN A STRANGE LAND	(03067-9—$1.95)
TIME ENOUGH FOR LOVE	(03471-2—$2.25)
TOMORROW THE STARS	(03432-1—$1.50)
THE UNPLEASANT PROFESSION OF JONATHAN HOAG	(03052-0—$1.50)

Send for a *free* list of all our books in print

These books are available at your local bookstore, or send price indicated plus 30¢ per copy to cover mailing costs to

Berkley Publishing Corporation
300 Murray Hill Parkway
East Rutherford, New Jersey 07073

EXCITING SCIENCE FICTION FROM BERKLEY BY CLIFFORD D. SIMAK

A CHOICE OF GODS	(03415-1—$1.25)
DESTINY DOLL	(02996-4—$1.25)
ENCHANTED PILGRIMAGE	(02987-5—$1.25)
THE GOBLIN RESERVATION	(03399-6—$1.25)
OUR CHILDREN'S CHILDREN	(02759-7—$.95)
OUT OF THEIR MINDS	(02997-2—$1.25)
SHAKESPEARE'S PLANET	(03394-5—$1.25)

Send for a *free* list of all our books in print

These books are available at your local bookstore, or send price indicated plus 30¢ per copy to cover mailing costs to

Berkley Publishing Corporation
300 Murray Hill Parkway
East Rutherford, New Jersey 07073